So
Jelly!

So
Jelly!

Coco Simon

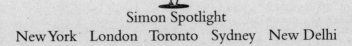

Simon Spotlight

New York   London   Toronto   Sydney   New Delhi

SIMON SPOTLIGHT
An imprint of Simon & Schuster Children's Publishing Division
1230 Avenue of the Americas, New York, New York 10020
This Simon Spotlight edition December 2019
Copyright © 2019 by Simon & Schuster, Inc.
All rights reserved, including the right of reproduction in whole or in part in any form.
SIMON SPOTLIGHT and colophon are registered trademarks of Simon & Schuster, Inc.
Text by Valerie Dobrow
For information about special discounts for bulk purchases, please contact Simon & Schuster Special Sales at 1-866-506-1949 or business@simonandschuster.com.
Designed by Ciara Gay
The text of this book was set in Bembo Std.
Manufactured in the United States of America 1019 OFF
10 9 8 7 6 5 4 3 2 1
ISBN 978-1-5344-6029-4 (hc)
ISBN 978-1-5344-6028-7 (pbk)
ISBN 978-1-5344-6030-0 (eBook)
Library of Congress Catalog Card Number 2019946642

Chapter One
I Don't Like Change

My friend Sophia was looking at me like I was crazy. "But you have a job!" she said. "That's so cool!"

I sighed and pushed my bangs off my face. They were really starting to annoy me, and I had to decide if I should just let them grow out or get them trimmed.

"Well, yes and no," I said. "Yes because it's cool to work at Donut Dreams, but no because it's hard work, and I'd rather be doing a lot of other things, like going out for pizza tomorrow with you."

I work at my family's restaurant, the Park View Table, after school Fridays and one day on the weekends. This week I'm working on Sunday.

Inside the Park there's a donut counter, Donut Dreams, that my grandmother started with her homemade donuts, which are kind of legendary around here. I work at the Donut Dreams counter with my cousin Lindsay.

Pretty much the rest of the family, from my sisters to my mom to my grandparents and everyone in between, also works at the Park. It's definitely a family business, and everyone in the family is expected to help out at the restaurant. We are paid, of course, but it's not like there's some discussion about where you want to work.

When Grandpa and Nans, which is what we call our grandmother, think that you're ready, you get offered a job, and then they figure out the best place for each of us in the restaurant. Saying something like, *No thanks, I'd rather lifeguard at the pool than work in the restaurant,* isn't really an option. Or at least no one has really tried.

I don't mind working with my family, but it's hard when my free time is eaten up by work while my friends get to hang out and do things—like how Sophia, Michelle, and Riley were planning to go out for pizza after school the next day.

"Hey! Are you coming with us tomorrow?" asked Riley as she plunked herself down at the lunch table.

"She's working," said Sophia with her mouth full.

"What?" said Riley, and then without waiting for an answer, she called out, "Oh hey, Isabella, over here!" Sophia and I looked up to see Isabella walking toward us.

We live in a small town called Bellgrove, which is the kind of place where everyone knows everyone else and always has. People rarely move here, so we've been in school with the same kids since kindergarten.

Poor Elizabeth Ellis is still known as "Wetsy Betsy" because she peed her pants in kindergarten. That's awful, and maybe I'd feel differently if I were Elizabeth, but I think it's still pretty nice to hang out with kids you've always known. So now that we're in middle school, it's not like there are suddenly any new kids around, but it seems like the groups of friends are changing.

Sophia, Michelle, Riley, and I have been what my dad calls "four peas in a pod" since we were toddlers. We have other friends too, but everyone knows we've always been a crew.

But when school started, Riley was suddenly really into hanging out with Isabella, who seems to be joining us at lunch on the regular.

Whenever I complain about having more people around instead of it just being the four of us, my mom always replies, "When it comes to friends, additions are always okay, but subtractions are not."

So I'm trying to be okay with more friends, but sometimes I'd like to subtract Isabella and just make it Sophia, Michelle, Riley, and me, like it always has been.

Sophia wrinkled her brow a little bit when Isabella sat next to Riley. No one else noticed, but if you've known her for eleven years like I have, you'd have noticed.

Michelle uses a wheelchair, and she wheeled her way over to my side. "Scootch over," she said, and I made room for her.

"Hey, Isabella," Sophia said.

Isabella put her tray down and looked like she was going to cry.

"What's wrong?" Sophia asked.

"You guys, I totally think I am going to fail my coding class," Isabella said. "I just do not get it."

"Bella, it's only the second month of school!" said Riley. "You'll get the hang of it." I had never really heard anyone call Isabella "Bella" before.

"Yeah, chill out, Isabella," Michelle said. "Take a deep breath. It's going to be fine."

"Ugh," said Isabella. "It's just so hard and there's so much pressure. I mean, they all say that everything starts to matter in middle school if you want to go to college!" she complained.

"You still have a long way until college!" I said. "No need to worry about it now. Trust me, my sister Jenna is in high school. That's when the pressure really starts."

That wasn't entirely accurate. Jenna had been talking about college for a good seven years. Jenna is the oldest of my siblings (she's a junior in high school) and a little bossy. Actually she's *a lot* bossy.

She and Lindsay, and even my adopted sister Molly, who is a few months older than me, are always talking about going away to college. My parents are okay with this, but I can tell they don't want us to go too far. Jenna talks about how she wants to go to a school in California, which kind of scares me.

She is also always talking about "getting away" from our small town, like it's some bad place to be. She loves reading about big cities or seeing movies that take place in big cities. One year for her birthday, Jenna asked for a bunch of travel guidebooks to all the big cities in the world, even though she's only been to one of them: Chicago.

I don't understand why you'd ever want to leave Bellgrove. This town is home to me. I mean, sure, it would be nice to go somewhere sometimes without being totally recognized, but then again, seeing familiar people is kind of nice.

I like that the person who cuts my hair has been cutting it since I was a baby; that the librarian, Ms. Castro, has known me since even before I could read; and that every year we do the same things, like go apple picking at Green Hills Orchards in September before we get the same hot apple cider at Corner Stop.

I like living within a few minutes of just about every single person in my extended family. All those things to me are not just dull things we're stuck with—they're traditions and familiar people and they make me feel safe.

I know I'll have to go to college in another town because there isn't a college here, but the closest state university, where my mom and dad and aunt and uncle went to school, is about two hours away. Mom keeps reassuring me that I can come home on the weekends if I want to.

When we have these conversations, Jenna just rolls her eyes and says, "Really, Kelsey? Stretch yourself! Open your eyes to new adventures! It's only two hours away!"

But to be honest, two hours away from *everything* I know sounds like plenty of an adventure for me.

"So," Sophia said, jolting me back to the table. "Are you going to try out for the field hockey team like we talked about?"

I nodded. "Yeah, it sounds fun, and Mom really wants me to do something active," I said.

Mom and Dad are always taking us on walks or bike rides, even when it's freezing cold outside. I wasn't too sure how I'd like playing competitively, but I love to be outside, especially in fall when the air turns crisp and smells so good.

"As long as I can still keep my hours working at the restaurant," I added.

"But your grandparents own the place where you work!" Riley said. "I'm guessing they can work with your schedule!"

"You'd think," I said, "but Grandpa is a stickler for

not giving us special consideration. We still have to clock in a certain amount of hours, unless our grades slip. School comes first."

"So if you fail a few tests, you can get out of work," snorted Isabella, or *Bella*.

"If I fail a few tests, I'd have a lot more to deal with than missing work," I retorted, kind of snapping at her. I don't know why, but Isabella gets under my skin sometimes.

"Well . . . ," said Riley. She paused, and Sophia and I looked up. "Bella and I were thinking about doing soccer instead of field hockey."

I caught Sophia's eyes, which looked as surprised as mine.

"That's great!" Michelle said. "So now I'll take photos of the soccer team as well as field hockey." Michelle takes awesome photos and dreams of being a professional photographer someday.

Riley bit her lip. "The thing is, I'm not sure I'm great at field hockey, and I know I'm a pretty good soccer player, so I want to try out for the team."

Isabella looked at her and smiled. I had a weird feeling they'd talked about this before. Sophia looked at me.

I shrugged. "Well, you should always do what makes you happy," I said. "Soph and I will be a team of two on the field hockey team."

Riley looked at me strangely. "Okay," she said. "I just don't want you guys to be disappointed that we all wouldn't be playing field hockey together. But you're right, you have each other on the field."

"Yep, we have each other," said Sophia.

It was quiet for a second, and then Michelle asked me, "So how is work going?"

I shrugged. "It's okay. A lot of the time I'd rather be somewhere else, but everyone in the family works there, so it's my turn to step up. Or at least that's what Grandpa said."

"Do you get to eat the extra donuts?" asked Isabella. "Because oh my goodness, I could eat, like, a dozen of those at a time."

"No," I said. "We donate the ones that haven't sold at the end of the day."

Sophia and I exchanged a smile, because everyone always asks me that question.

People think if you work at a donut shop you eat donuts all day, every day. In elementary school, Joshua Victor asked me if our house was made of donuts.

"Well, you've been known to show up with donuts," teased Riley, and I laughed.

I do try to bring donuts to my friends' houses when we have extra or when Mom brings them home.

"Work perk!" I said.

"Oh, I can almost taste those cider donuts," moaned Isabella. "Shoot, now all I want is a cider donut. It's definitely better than . . . whatever this lunch they're serving is."

"My favorites are the coffee-cake donuts," Michelle said. "And the chocolate ones with rainbow sprinkles. Or the plain glazed ones. Or . . . "

"We get it. You like donuts!" Riley said with a laugh.

Just then the bell rang. We gathered up our stuff and hustled out to our next class.

As we were going into the hall, Sophia grabbed my arm and hissed, "What is going on with Riley?"

I sighed and shrugged. "She *is* really good at soccer," I said.

"Well, Riley may be good at soccer, but she'd better be good at being our friend," said Sophia, and before I could respond, she shot off down the hall.

So Jelly!

Isabella, Riley, and Michelle turned in a different direction, heading toward language arts, where they were in a class with my sister Molly. Before they went into their class, I caught Molly's eye as she walked by in the hallway.

It was obvious she could tell something was up. She was looking at me as if to ask, *What's going on?*

But I just said, "You'd better catch up to your potential new soccer teammates," and hurried off to my own class.

Middle school was different, that's for sure, and I don't think I like change.

Chapter Two
Sisterly Love

My dad is usually home after school. He teaches woodshop at the high school during the year, and in the summer he works for a construction company that his brother owns.

Molly and I dumped our stuff in the cubbies that he built us, kind of like lockers, near the back door and found him in the kitchen, making a snack.

You'd think that because Mom's family owns a restaurant she'd be a really good cook, but she totally is not. She jokes that's why she married Dad, because he can whip up anything and it's always delicious.

I sniffed. "Ooh, popcorn!"

"And hello to you too, honey," said Dad.

He was popping kernels in a deep pot on the

stove, and the kitchen smelled like a movie theater. He pushed a plate of sliced bananas and peanut butter toward us.

"Dad, where are the raisins on top?" Molly asked.

Dad used to call this snack "ants on a log," which we thought was hysterical. He slices the bananas lengthwise, smears on peanut butter, then scatters raisins on top. He used to tell us that they were ants crawling on a banana log. We thought it was funny, but it could also explain why I hate raisins . . . I mean, eww, eating ants! I always pick them off.

"We're out," said Dad. "It's still back-to-school season, and Mom and I have been so crazed and busy we haven't been able to get to the market."

"So, ant-less?" asked Molly.

"Yes, I'm afraid we are out of ants, Molls," said Dad. "So I am making it up to you with some popcorn."

"If we put these on top . . . ," said Molly, cocking her head and thinking.

"They could be clouds on a log," I said, taking a piece of hot popcorn.

"They could be fluffy sheep on a log," said Molly. "That makes more sense. Why would clouds be on a log?"

13

Dad grabbed the grocery list that Mom kept on the fridge door and wrote *raisins* on it.

"Okay, I'm still finishing up this summer job and I have to install the cabinets I built," he said. "So I'm going to head out until dinnertime."

This year Mom and Dad have been letting us stay in the house without them home, but only during the day. Dad is always here after school, though, which is nice, even if he's sometimes really annoying and asks a ton of questions about our day.

Today, though, Dad was in a hurry.

"Okay, dinner is in the slow cooker," he said, "so whatever you do, do not turn that thing off, or we'll all starve. Mom will be home by five thirty. We both have our phones at the ready, so just text or call if you need anything."

"Where's Jenna?" I asked.

"At work," said Dad. "Wait, is she at work? This new schedule . . . ," he muttered.

He scurried over to the bulletin board in the kitchen, where Mom keeps a monthly calendar and writes down who goes where on each day. Dad calls it the Command Center.

"Yep, yep, she went to work after she had a

student council meeting, and Mom will bring her home when her shift ends," said Dad.

"Dad, did you just lose track of a daughter?" teased Molly.

"No!" said Dad, but we all laughed.

Mom is crazy detail-oriented. Everything at home is organized beyond belief. Like the cans in our kitchen cabinets are basically alphabetized. Her socks are folded a certain way and arranged by color. Maybe it's because she's an accountant, and, as she says, accountants have to be precise about things because they work with numbers.

As the accountant for the restaurant, she makes sure that all the finances are up to date, like the staff gets paid, the bills are paid on time, and at the end of the month the restaurant isn't spending more money than it's making.

Uncle Charlie does all the ordering, everything from napkins to food to supplies like extra water glasses, because in a restaurant you are always breaking glasses. Uncle Mike runs Donut Dreams, where I work. Nans plans out the menus and figures out the daily specials, and makes her special donuts, and Grandpa . . . well, as Grandpa proudly tells everyone, he steers the ship and keeps it on course.

Everyone has their "own lane" as they all like to say, and they say that a lot to each other, as in "Hey, get out of my lane!" when they step on each other's toes. Everyone has a different role, but we all work together.

Dad builds things, so he has to be precise too, but in a really different way. When he's building something, he's all about measuring, and remeasuring, and cutting things accurately so everything fits together.

But when he isn't building something he isn't too precise, which drives Mom crazy. Once he went to pick me up at dance class . . . only I wasn't at dance class, I was waiting for him to pick me up at the library. He also once dropped off Molly for a playdate at the wrong house.

He's always messing up the laundry, too. Just last week Jenna was struggling and trying to get into a pair of jeans until she realized that they were mine; Dad had put them away in her closet instead.

"I have it together!" said Dad, a little indignantly.

"Okay," said Molly. "So you know you have to take me to soccer, right?"

"What?" said Dad, looking panicked.

"Practice starts at six," said Molly. "It's on the board!"

Dad went over to the bulletin board. "Oh … yeah, there it is."

Just then our phones lit up with a text message from Mom.

> All good? Everyone home?

"It's like she senses when we need her," said Molly, laughing.

"She probably just wants to check in to see how school was," said Dad.

He texted back,

> All OK.

Molly added,

> Dad forgot soccer.

About two seconds later, Mom called Dad's phone.

He picked up immediately and reassured her that everything was fine and that he would be home in time to get Molly to soccer, and that he would take me with him if she wasn't home from work yet.

He then left the house to finish his work, and the house was nice and quiet.

Not that my older sister Jenna or Dad or Mom are loud people, but you notice when they are around. I can always hear Mom puttering around the house, or Jenna playing music.

Sometimes I even hear Molly practicing with her soccer ball against a wall somewhere, stopping only when Mom or Dad yells, "Molly, cut it out!"

I wondered if our house would still be like this once Jenna left for college, when it would just be the four of us. It seems so weird that she wouldn't be here every day. The thing about having two sisters is that you get really used to having them around.

"Do you ever wonder what it will be like when Jenna moves out?" I asked Molly, who was sitting right next to me at the counter.

"What?" she asked, looking up from her phone.

"When Jenna goes to college," I said, a little annoyed that she wasn't listening. "When it's just the four of us instead of five, do you worry that it will be weird?"

Molly wrinkled her forehead. "I dunno," she said. "Like will we miss her?"

"Well, we'll miss her, sure," I said. "But I mean, what will dinner be like without her? What will the weekends be like?"

"Well, the weekends will be easier, because we don't have to worry about making noise and waking her up," said Molly, in her very matter-of-fact Molly way.

This was true. Jenna liked to sleep in on the weekends, and she was always barking at us to keep it down. Molly and I are early risers.

"But won't it be like one person is just missing?" I asked.

I knew Molly wasn't always into these kinds of conversations, so I was pushing it.

"Things change, Kelsey," Molly said in a tone that sounded like she was explaining it to a two-year-old.

"Oh, never mind," I said, and pushed away my chair. Molly was making me feel worse instead of better.

Sometimes getting people to talk in our family was impossible. My cousin Lindsay was the one I used to talk to about everything. We're just about the same age and grew up together, so in a lot of ways we are more like sisters than cousins.

But Lindsay's mom, my aunt Amy, died a couple years ago after being sick for a long time. If you talk to Lindsay, she doesn't burst into tears or anything, or at least not usually, but I'm always really careful when I talk to her now, especially if I'm talking about my family.

If, say, I complain about Mom, I'm worried that Lindsay is really thinking, *Oh, well, at least you still have your mom.* If I tried to talk to her about how weird it would be with Jenna gone, I'm afraid she would think, *Well, she's just going to college. She's coming back. But my mom isn't.*

Lindsay is actually really sweet, so I don't think she'd think those things on purpose, and she would never say them to me out loud, but there are things I just can't talk to her about anymore.

"You'd better get your homework started before Mom gets home," said Molly.

I looked over, annoyed, and I noticed that while I'd been sitting there thinking, she had already set up her laptop and was typing away.

Molly is only eight months older than I am, but

she acts like she is my much older sister. So between her and Jenna, I really feel ganged up on sometimes and like I am the baby of the family.

Jenna and Molly are a lot alike. They are both super organized and they belong to a million different clubs and are always thinking about their next project or what they'll be doing in ten years.

Dad calls me Kelsey Dreamer because I guess I daydream a lot, and I like to take my time doing things. I just don't feel that crazy rushing sense or the competitiveness that Jenna and Molly seem to have been born with.

I opened my laptop, logged in, and clicked over to the homework page and sighed. Ugh. There is *so* much homework in middle school. There was no way I'd finish before dinner, which I hated. I liked to be able to relax after dinner, and have what Dad calls downtime, when you kind of just do nothing.

I peeked over at Molly. "Do we have to read this whole chapter for history?" I asked.

"Yes," said Molly, her hands flying over the keyboard.

I opened the window and breathed in. "Ooh, someone is burning leaves," I said. I love that smell.

I positioned my chair so the breeze from outside tickled my face. It was a shame to spend such a beautiful afternoon inside doing homework.

Then I looked over at Molly again. "Did you finish reading it already?" I asked.

"Yeeesss," said Molly with a hint of annoyance, not looking up from her laptop.

"What is it about?" I asked.

"KELSEY!" Molly screamed so loud I jumped. "You have to do your own homework! I'm not going to do it for you!"

"I wasn't asking you to do my homework," I said crossly. "I was just curious."

"If you're curious, then open the book," said Molly, and she sounded exactly like Mom when she said it.

I sat there for a few more minutes, listening to the leaves crinkle in the wind. Dad was going to make us help rake them up on the weekend.

"Kelsey, I can help you if you get stuck, but you have to start and you have to try," said Molly.

"Okay," I said, eating some more popcorn. "This tastes so much better when Dad makes it on the stove than in the microwave," I said. "And it's fluffier."

Molly looked at me sideways. "Thanks for the review, Princess Popcorn," she said.

I snickered.

Molly looked over and giggled too. Then she grabbed a handful and chewed. "You're right," she said. "This does taste good."

She glanced over at me with a mischievous twinkle in her eye that I know well and said, "Sheep on a log! Well, what if those sheep *flew*?"

Then she hurled a fistful of popcorn at me.

"MOLLY!" I screamed, shaking popcorn from my hair but laughing.

I tossed some down the back of her shirt.

"Oh, it is *on*, Princess Popcorn!" she said, and showered me with half of what was in the bowl.

We were both throwing the popcorn and cracking up when we heard my mom say, loudly, "Girls, what on earth is going on in here?"

Jenna peered around her. "Are you maniacs having a popcorn fight?"

We both said, "No!" while popcorn fell from our hair, and we tried not to giggle.

Mom sighed and handed me the broom and Molly the dustpan. "I don't even want to know. And

I don't want to see anything either . . . please clean up this mess."

I started sweeping and Molly scooped up the piles, but we couldn't stop laughing.

"Sheep on a log!" Molly whispered, trying to stifle her laughter.

"What are sheep on a log?" asked Jenna.

"What happens when you don't have ants," I said, and Molly started to laugh even harder.

"What?" asked Jenna, but she started to laugh too.

Sometimes that happens when we're all together. We just start laughing and we can't stop, sometimes over something silly and sometimes over nothing at all.

Mom looked at the three of us cackling and threw up her hands. "I don't get it," she said. "But the sound of you three girls laughing is always the best."

Molly and I settled down and cleaned up and Jenna started to set the table. I felt another surge— this was so nice—the three of us together with our own secret kind of language.

Why would you ever want to leave it? I just wished it could stay this way forever.

Chapter Three
Morning Meeting Surprise

Every day at school we have the morning meeting in the cafeteria. All the classes gather there and we hang out until Principal Clarke stands up and reads any announcements or talks about upcoming events.

I headed over to the corner table where I always sat with Sophia, Michelle, and Riley, and I was surprised to see Isabella sitting there already.

"Good morning!" she said, smiling at me.

I looked around, thinking it was odd that she wasn't sitting with Olivia, whom she was normally always with.

"Hi!" I said, and dropped my backpack on the table.

Isabella was best friends with Olivia. They'd been

inseparable all summer long and they'd join us at the lake, usually with Hannah and Elizabeth, too. I hadn't really seen the two of them hanging out much since school started, though. . . .

Casey and my cousin Lindsay sat across from us. Casey and Lindsay had been BFFs since they were babies. We're all still friends with each other, but we all have certain friends we're closer to than others. Or at least we used to.

"How was soccer?" I asked Isabella.

"Oh, Riley didn't tell you?" she said.

Again, I got this short-tempered feeling. It wasn't like she'd said anything bad or wrong, but it was just the fact that she said it that bothered me.

"No, that's why I'm asking you," I said.

"Oh," said Isabella, either not noticing I was annoyed or ignoring me. "She did really great. She was on a scrimmage team with Molly."

I wondered why Molly hadn't mentioned it.

Riley bounded in, chomping on a bagel, with Sophia in tow. Riley was a total talk-fest, while Sophia and I were usually quieter until we got going. We're both early risers but not naturally enthusiastic morning people.

"Hey, Bella Bella!" Riley chimed.

Sophia and I looked at each other, annoyed at her perkiness.

A minute or two later Hannah sat down with us, and so did Elizabeth. We all paused for a moment while Elizabeth unpacked her food. Her mom made her the most awesome sandwiches and salads.

Every time my grandfather would see Elizabeth at the restaurant, he would remind her to tell her mom there's always a job open for her as a chef if she wants one.

Elizabeth smiled at all of us as she took out her sandwich.

"Nothing very exotic this morning," she informed us. "Cream cheese on date nut bread."

"That's exotic to me," Michelle said. "I've never had cream cheese on anything but a bagel!"

"The crunchy nuts are good with the cream cheese," Elizabeth said.

We all chatted about our food for a few minutes when suddenly Hannah cleared her throat dramatically so we all turned to look at her.

"So, I'm running for student council," she said, whipping her phone out. "And in order to run, I need twenty-five signatures to get on the ballot."

"I'll sign," said Sophia, and took Hannah's phone. "Wait . . . you're running with Olivia?"

"Yeah!" said Hannah. "Olivia is my running mate. Our campaign slogan is 'Two Girls Can Get It Done!'"

"I didn't know you guys were that friendly," I said.

"What do you mean?" said Hannah. She waved her hand around. "We've all known each other since kindergarten!"

That was true. But when did Hannah even start talking to Olivia, let alone hanging out with her? We'd all hung out at the lake together this past summer, but I'd never noticed Hannah and Olivia being particularly buddy-buddy.

"You need a campaign plan," said Riley, signing after Sophia. "We should talk about it after school when we go for pizza."

"But Kelsey can't come," said Michelle. "She has to work."

They all looked at me.

"Sorry," I said, looking down at the phone and signing my name.

Part of me wasn't so mad that I had to work. I

wasn't sure about all this new student council stuff or hanging out with Olivia, Isabella, Hannah, and Elizabeth instead of just Sophia, Michelle, and Riley.

"Good morning, ladies and gentlemen," said Principal Clarke into the microphone.

The room settled down.

"Today we have to report that a lost gray sweatshirt was left in the STEAM lab. If it's yours, please come to the office during lunch."

"Oh that's mine!" yelled Jeff Simons, and everyone laughed.

"Okay, Jeff. You can pick it up later," said Principal Clarke. "Also, we have some exciting new programs this year. We've decided that we are going to elect class representatives for each grade, one student per grade.

"And this position will be different from student council. Our representatives will actually be representing their classes with the teachers and working on how to improve your school day. So think of your rep as your human suggestion box.

"The idea is that you can go to your rep with issues or concerns or questions, and your rep will bring them to a committee that some teachers and

I will be on to make decisions about your concerns.

"The rep should be someone who is a good listener, who can work with many groups of people, and who is enthusiastic about our time at Bellgrove Middle School. We have nominations that will go in the ballot box in the cafeteria.

"If you know of someone you think can best represent your class, please write down their name and submit it to us. The results will be announced next Friday."

There was a lot of conversation and murmuring. Lindsay and Casey nodded at each other and then looked at me.

"Our grade representative should be you, Kelsey," Casey said.

"ME?" I looked at them, stunned. "Why?"

"Well," said Lindsay, "you get along with everyone, and you're a pretty good student."

She cleared her throat, because she knew I'd had a lot of trouble with social studies last year.

"And you really do always know the right thing to say. Also, if it's supposed to be someone who loves BMS, well, anytime anyone says something bad about Bellgrove, you always say how wonderful it is. You should be, like, the spokesperson for living here."

I knew that Lindsay, like Jenna, couldn't wait to get out of Bellgrove, so I wasn't quite sure if she was complimenting me or if she was shading me just a little bit.

Sophia put her arm around me. "You are the best representative for everything, Kels," she said.

"Absolutely!" said Riley. "I vote for Kelsey!"

I smiled.

You can always rely on your BFFs. Even when they try out for the soccer team.

Chapter Four
A Bad Day At Work

As far as jobs at the Park go, working at the Donut Dreams counter is one of the easiest, and I think that's why they gave it to Lindsay, then just paired me with her. It's not that everyone always just gives Lindsay a pass. I mean, she does have to work, but it's like everyone in our family tries to make things a lot easier for her if they can.

After Aunt Amy died, Mom sat us down and talked about how we'd need to be sensitive around Lindsay. And while I totally get that, I also wonder when we won't have to tiptoe around her anymore, and when things can finally go back to normal.

I was in a little bit of a sour mood when I arrived

at the Park, because I knew Sophia and Riley and Michelle were out for pizza and I had to work.

Michelle had texted me,

Wish u were here!

She had also sent a selfie of her taking a huge bite out of the most amazing slice of pepperoni pizza I had ever seen. My mouth had watered just looking at it.

Guess I looked more grouchy than I thought, because when I walked in, tying my apron behind me, Grandpa boomed, "What's wrong? Aren't you glad to be at work today, my lovely Kelsey?"

He was standing at the front podium of the restaurant. A podium is kind of funny, when you think about it, because we have one at school. It's like a stand that they roll out when we have an assembly or a speaker, and the speaker stands behind it.

We have one at the restaurant, because that's where the host stands. The host greets everyone who comes in and asks how many people are in their party (which also makes me giggle, because how is going out for lunch a party?), and then shows them to their table.

My cousin Lily is the host a lot because she's really friendly and patient with people. She's also not the *best* waitress because she's a little clumsy, so they had to find another job for her.

I sighed. "Well, I'm coming to work on a beautiful day, Grandpa," I said.

"And?" he bellowed.

"And my friends all went out for pizza after school and I had to come to work," I said, frowning. I knew I sounded a little bratty, but I couldn't help it.

"Some people would be very glad to have a job, Ms. Kelsey," said Grandpa. "You are lucky to be able to start making money to save for college."

College. Again. Why was everyone so obsessed with college?

"And," he said, "that's why they call it work and not play. Just like homework. They don't call it 'homeplay,' do they?"

I shook my head.

"Now, try not to look so grumpy," said Grandpa. "Customers don't like buying a sweet donut from a grumpy server!"

I blew the bangs off my forehead. They were annoying me today too.

So Jelly!

I forced a smile at Grandpa and walked over to the Donut Dreams counter, where Lindsay was already wiping down the glass case.

"Hi," I said unenthusiastically.

"Bad mood?" asked Lindsay.

"Yeah," I said, and then I regretted it.

I mean, what did I really have to be in a bad mood about in front of Lindsay? I still had my mom and dad and everyone was healthy.

I put my phone under the counter, as we had to do when we were working. Grandpa was a real stickler about that.

"How busy are we?" I asked Lindsay, who was making sure all the trays were filled and neat.

"Not too bad," she said. "I got here a little early and there were some high school kids, but not a huge crowd."

I leaned on the counter, which was another Grandpa "no-no." You were always supposed to look "alert and approachable," according to the rules. Grandpa had *a lot* of rules at the restaurant.

When you started working at the Park and at Donut Dreams, you got a little employee handbook with all the rules listed. Most of them were pretty obvious, like always wash your hands, which is reasonable if you are serving food (because eeeeuuw!), but some of them were a pain: no cell phones, no leaning, say hello to everyone you see, no eating in the dining area of the restaurant—only in the kitchen. Grandpa thought it looked sloppy to have the employees shoving food in their mouths or dropping crumbs all over the place.

Sometimes Lindsay and I snuck a donut under the counter if we were really slow. It is hard to be around them all day without wanting just a little bite, but usually by the end of my shifts, I never want to see or smell a donut again.

Mom came out of the back room, where her office was, and waved at me.

"Ah, I wanted to make sure Jenna dropped you off," she said.

"I'm here," I said.

Mom frowned. "Did you have a bad day?"

"No," I said, not really wanting to get into it.

Mom looked at me for a second, paused, then gave me a quick kiss on the head. Then she went over to Lindsay and gave her a quick kiss too.

"How was your day, honey?" she asked.

Lindsay smiled. "It was okay," she said, "but we have tons of homework over the weekend!"

"That's middle school for you," said Mom. "Hey, did Nans talk to you about starting piano lessons?"

Lindsay shook her head.

"Okay," said Mom. "Because your dad said you were interested, so I'm trying to find a teacher who can come to the house."

"Cool," said Lindsay. "Thanks, Aunt Melissa."

I wondered why Mom was busy trying to find a piano teacher for Lindsay.

Nans and Grandpa were always around, so they could help out. So that meant that Lindsay and her brother, Skylar, had three people looking after them, plus Mom. Jenna, Molly, and I only had Mom and Dad, and they were barely hanging on with how busy they were.

"Okay, girls, have a good shift," said Mom. "I've got to get back to work. Wait . . ." She turned around. "Did you girls have a snack after school?"

"Nans packed me some peanut butter crackers," said Lindsay.

Mom looked at me. "Did Dad give you anything?"

"Well, all we had were graham crackers, since no

one had time to go to the supermarket this week," I pouted.

Mom looked a little annoyed at my pout. "Well, luckily you work in a restaurant with a pretty extensive menu. What do you want?"

"Nothing," I said. "I'm not hungry."

I knew I was acting a little snotty and I didn't even really know why, but I still couldn't help myself.

Mom sighed and I could tell she was about to say something, but then she changed her mind.

"Okay, well, I'm here if you need me," she said, and then headed back to her office.

Lindsay and I wiped the shelves down in silence, then swept the floor behind the counter. Then we ran out of things to do, so we just tried to look busy.

The after-school crowd comes in various waves. Grandpa usually shuffles some people around and has one of the waitresses work the donut counter to serve some of the kids before Lindsay and I get there.

"I didn't know you wanted to take piano lessons," I finally said.

Lindsay shrugged. "Yeah, well, Dad keeps telling me I need more activities. And I don't really like any sports, so we figured music might be good. Hey, speaking of sports, do you have field hockey tryouts tomorrow?"

"No tryouts yet," I said, "Practice starts tomorrow, and we scrimmage so they can watch everyone. Then they do the observations and decide who makes the team."

I heard the bell ring when the front door to the restaurant opened, and a pack of kids came swarming in and made a beeline for the Donut Dreams counter.

"Brace yourself," I said.

"Oh boy," said Lindsay. "Here come the East twins."

For the next half hour we were slammed, with kids whining, "That one . . . no, no, that one," as our hands hovered over exactly which donut they wanted.

Freddy Benson had a fit, claiming that his sister got a bigger donut than he did, even though they were exactly the same.

One mom came in with two little girls. They had enormous blue eyes and hair so blond it almost looked white. They looked like two tiny angels—sweet and innocent.

One of the girls asked me for a chocolate glazed donut, "with extra sprinkles, please." The second girl wanted a jelly donut. Their mom looked exhausted and just ordered a coffee.

I handed the first girl her chocolate donut, heaped with sprinkles.

She thanked me politely and then promptly smashed the donut into her sister's hair and face. "That's for losing my Barbie," she yelled.

Her sister screamed and then threw *her* donut at her sister, before anyone could stop her.

Grandpa was there immediately to help clean up.

"That's a waste of two delicious donuts, young ladies," he said to the girls.

He was trying to look stern, but I saw he was trying really hard not to laugh.

Their mom was mortified and kept apologizing.

Grandpa waved his hand as if to say, *Don't worry about it*, and then gave the mom an old-fashioned donut on the house.

Another mother was leaving the restaurant area when both of her kids (a boy and a girl) spotted the Donut Dreams counter and started chanting, "Donuts! Donuts! Dooo-nuts!"

The mom sighed heavily and said, "Donuts aren't really good for you."

"They are good for the soul," Lindsay said seriously.

"And for your tummy!" I said, laughing.

"You know what they say," Grandpa said, joining the conversation. "You can be sad before you eat a donut. And you can be sad after you eat a donut. But nobody is ever sad *while* they are eating a donut!"

The mom laughed and said to her children, "All right. Just this once!"

The kids whooped and cheered as they picked out their treats.

"Oh, they'll be back," Grandpa said with a smile.

Lindsay and I looked at each other after the line finally died down and said, "Whoa" at the same time.

I started sweeping up all the sprinkle crumbs on the floor, and she was wiping down the small tables and chairs that we have right next to the counter.

We almost had everything back to normal when Uncle Mike, Lindsay's dad, came over.

"Hey, girls," he said. "Listen, Skylar has an earache and I need to run him over to the doctor." He looked a little worried. "Nans is with him in the car out front but he doesn't want Nans to take him, so she'll come here and will step in if anything comes up for you."

"Poor Sky," said Lindsay.

Skylar can be an enormous pain, but he's also really cute. I flinched because I used to get earaches all the time and they were really painful.

Lindsay and I watched as Uncle Mike switched spots with Nans in the car outside, and Nans headed into the restaurant.

I almost said, *Poor kid probably just wants his mom*, which is what I want when I get sick, but I caught myself just in time.

"How are my girls?" asked Nans.

"Selling lots of donuts today!" said Lindsay.

"Excellent!" said Nans. She came over and gave me a little hug. "Always happy to see my girls hard at work."

She went over to talk to Grandpa, then headed into the kitchen.

At the end of the day's shift, we need to use the iPad and enter in all the sales. That automatically adds up how many donuts we sold and how much money we should have in the cash drawer. If the cash drawer doesn't match the receipts, there can be a big problem.

Then we pack up all the extra donuts. Every night Grandpa drops them off at the police station, the firehouse, and the senior center, so we divide them into three boxes. If there aren't enough to fill three boxes, then Grandpa puts in some cake or pie so everyone still gets some goodies. As we packed up the boxes at the end of our shift, I started to relax a little bit from the week.

We have something called Family of Five Fridays. Every Friday all five of us are home for an early dinner together, and after dinner we all either watch a movie or play a game. We've been doing it ever since I can remember. Jenna tried to get out of it a few times to go out with her friends, but Mom and Dad put their foot down, and she stopped trying. Sometimes we can hang out with friends after school, but we can't miss dinner.

We were just about done with the boxes when Mom came over with her keys in her hand. "When you're done closing, just let Nans know," she said. "I'll be waiting outside."

"Is Nans taking me home?" asked Lindsay.

"Oh!" said Mom. "Didn't Mike tell you? You're coming home for dinner with us tonight. That way your dad can get Sky in bed and we can try to make sure you don't get sick too. We'll run you home after we're done with game night."

"Oh," said Lindsay, and she didn't seem sad exactly, just kind of uncertain.

So now Lindsay was barging in on Family of Five Friday. I knew it wasn't nice, but that made me even more crabby. Family of Five Fridays was about *our* family of five. It wasn't about "additional guests." Like I said, I don't deal well with change.

I sighed.

Why couldn't anything just stay the same?

Chapter Five
Not a Team Player

I got up early on Saturday like I usually do. Jenna is the only one in our family who sleeps in on weekends.

The rest of us are early risers, and when I got downstairs, Mom and Dad had already gone for their run and Molly was sitting at the table reading a book, dressed in her soccer outfit.

"Does anyone know I have field hockey today?" I asked, and Molly looked up.

"Is it on the board?" she asked.

I looked. "Yeah."

"Then they know. Or at least Mom does."

I sighed, poured myself a glass of orange juice, and sat down.

On Saturdays Mom doesn't have to be in the

office, so she and Dad go for their run, and then we have a big breakfast.

"Why were you in such a bad mood last night?" Molly asked.

"I wasn't," I lied.

"You were," said Molly matter-of-factly.

She turned the page of her book. Molly was always able to do more than one thing at a time.

"And honestly, I'm not sure you were too friendly to Lindsay," she added

"I don't think I was *un*friendly," I said.

I just kind of ignored Lindsay. Which you could say wasn't very friendly. I was just so mad to have her crash our Family Friday night.

"So what's up?" Molly asked.

I decided not to answer her and went upstairs to get dressed for field hockey. I had played last year, but it was basically just for fun. I wasn't sure what to expect with something more competitive.

I texted Sophia to see what she was wearing, then settled on shorts, a T-shirt, and a sweatshirt, since it was getting a little chilly this time of year. I put my hair in a ponytail and looked at my face in the mirror.

Jenna started wearing a little makeup in high

school, but Mom was really strict about what she could wear.

I noticed that some of the girls in my class were wearing makeup this year. It was weird: the day before school started, nobody was wearing any makeup when we were at the lake, and then the next day at school, a lot of girls just showed up with lip gloss and mascara and even, in the case of Marina Miles, blush.

I didn't think I could push it, and it was just field hockey practice, so I brushed my hair out, put on a little bit of the pink lip gloss Jenna had given me, and went downstairs.

"Are you wearing lip gloss to hockey practice?" asked Molly. My sister does not miss a thing.

"No," I said sarcastically. "My lips are naturally this shiny and pink."

She scowled at me.

Mom and Dad came through the side door, panting and laughing.

"I was not that slow today," said Dad.

Mom shook her head. "Your pace was off," she said. "It was like running with a turtle."

Everyone in my family was active, which was great, but they were also competitive. Mom and Dad didn't just go on a weekly run together, they actually raced each other.

Molly was a little nuts about soccer and always played in the competitive league, and Jenna is one of the stars on the tennis team and is always talking about her form. She's a great player, but she can be a little annoying when she talks about tennis.

Me, well, I like sports and I like to play, but I don't always care who wins the game. So I wasn't really nervous about field hockey, just more curious about what it would be like.

Dad took a quick shower and drove me to the town field where everybody goes to practice.

"Do you want me to stay?" he asked as I opened the car door.

"You don't have to," I said. "But it ends at noon, so can you pick me up then?"

"I'll be here!" said Dad.

He waited until I trotted over to the field and then waved and drove off.

Sophia was waiting for me on the field, as planned. Hannah was already there talking to her, and I spotted Olivia walking toward them. I could also see Michelle already snapping tons of photos from the sidelines. It was an all-middle-school team, so there were also a lot of older girls who were hanging out together.

Hannah waved to Olivia, and Olivia walked over to us.

"Hi," she said shyly. "Anyone else a little nervous?"

Hannah looked around. "Well, if it's just the four of us and they need representation from every class, it looks like we're in without even having to show them we know how to hold a stick!"

We all laughed.

"Oh, speaking of representation," said Olivia. "I nominated you, Kelsey, for the class representative."

"You did?" I said, surprised.

"Yeah, I asked Casey, and she said she and Lindsay were suggesting you to everyone because you're such a good listener. And Lindsay said you were really supportive, too."

"She's the best listener," said Sophia, flinging her arm around me. "I'd vote for her for anything!"

"Oh speaking of voting," I said. "Olivia, I hear you're running for student council with Hannah."

"Yes! Vote for us!" said Hannah, smiling.

"Well, the two of you have my vote too," I said.

"Thanks!" said Olivia. "That means a lot."

She said it really warmly, and I realized that maybe she was nice. Maybe it was just that I didn't know her well enough before.

"Hey, we should post pictures of our practice on our campaign page," suggested Hannah.

She took out her phone, and she and Olivia grinned for a selfie.

"I'll caption this, 'We're on the team and we are a team!'" Hannah said.

"Oh, that's good!" said Olivia. "But we're not on the team yet."

Coach Wickstead blew her whistle. "Okay, girls!" she shouted.

She called us over, then split us into teams of six so we could play three on three. Then she divided the field and assigned us our spot.

I was paired with two older girls, Amanda and Tracey. Amanda took charge and dropped the ball and we started to play.

I noticed that she grunted a lot and would mutter, "Pass, pass," or "Defense," either to herself or to one of us, I wasn't even sure. It was kind of annoying.

We took a water break and all sat on the side of the field. It was one of those perfect fall days where it was warm and sunny but there was a little bit of a breeze.

Say what you will about being stuck in a small town, like Jenna and Lindsay do, but we were stuck in a beautiful town, that's for sure. The old oak trees around the field were thick and tall, and you could hear the brook behind them actually bubbling. There was blue sky forever. If you leaned back and looked up, it felt like you were inside a big, blue snow globe.

The whistle blew again and we finished our last scrimmage. Coach Wickstead had us log our stats at the end of the practice.

Amanda wrote ours down. "Don't worry," she said to me. "This is just the first practice."

I was surprised, because I hadn't really been worried. I mean, I hadn't scored, but I didn't think I'd played badly.

As we were walking to the parking lot, I told Sophia what Amanda had said.

"Oh, she's the star player," she said. "She lives and breathes field hockey. Don't mind her."

Dad was waiting by the car, watching my cousin Rich practice lacrosse on the field next to us. He waved to Rich, then turned to me.

"How'd it go, kiddo?" he asked.

"It was okay," I said. "Next practice is Monday."

"I didn't want to hover," said Dad, "or make you nervous."

"Why would I be nervous?" I asked. "It was just a practice! Plus, it was fun!"

"Well," said Dad. "You know the coaches are still watching to see where the strengths are and who might play each position. Plus, Jenna . . ."

"Oh, well, Jenna is kind of nuts about that stuff," I said.

"Yes, she is," said Dad. "But she's conditioned us!"

Jenna is insanely superstitious about who comes to her matches, where we sit, and even, one year, what Mom wears.

Jenna had won a really tough match one time when Mom was wearing a sweatshirt, and Jenna made Mom wear that same sweatshirt to every match she had for the rest of the season. By the last match we called it the "stinky sweatshirt," even though Mom swore she washed it after each wear. It's totally bonkers.

We drove over to Molly's soccer practice, and Dad and I sat on the bleachers, watching. Molly liked Dad to watch her practices and games, and they always talked about them afterward.

I spotted Riley and Isabella on the field. Riley was right; she was really good, and pretty confident on the field. She and Molly were passing the ball back and forth, smiling at each other and nodding.

Then she and Isabella passed the ball back and forth. Isabella wasn't as fast or as great with her foot skills, which for some reason made me just a little happy. Maybe she wouldn't make the team.

"Wow, I didn't know Riley was playing soccer instead of hockey with you," Dad said.

"Yeah," I said, and stopped. I didn't know if I felt like getting into it.

"So some of the peas in the pod split?" Dad asked, clearly wanting to know more.

"We didn't split," I said testily. "Riley just thinks she's better at soccer, that's all."

Dad looked at me closely but didn't push it. Instead he said, "I was just making a little joke. Split peas . . . get it?"

I groaned.

"Hiya!" Riley waved to us as the practice ended. "How was hockey?"

"It was okay," I said. "You looked good."

"Did I?" Riley asked, and grinned. "That's good to hear. Your sister is a real monster out there. I hope I can keep up with her."

"If I don't get home and eat lunch, I'm going to eat the car," said Molly.

"Let's go, girls," said Dad. "I can afford lunch, but I can't afford another car!"

Jenna was sitting at the kitchen table, scrolling through her phone, when we came inside.

"How was hockey?" she asked.

"Fine," I said. "It was a nice morning to be outside."

Jenna looked at me strangely. "Well, yes, but how did you do in the practice?"

"Okay, I guess," I said.

"How were the other girls?" asked Dad.

He was making himself more coffee as Molly made a peanut butter sandwich.

"They're good," I said.

"Last year they had really good offense but not such a great defensive line," said Molly. "Is Amanda playing this year?"

"Yes," I said. "She was on my scrimmage team."

"Oh wow," said Jenna, "so they paired you with the star. That's a good sign."

"A sign of what?" I asked.

"That you'll make the team," said Jenna, speaking slowly.

"Oh, I'll make the team," I said. "There are only four girls from my year trying out. They'll use us somehow."

"But you might not get to play," said Molly.

"Eh," I said. "I don't mind. I still get to play in the practices. Besides, the games might be too much pressure."

"Kelsey, are you sure you even want to be on the team?" asked Dad. "If you want to play and not compete, you can probably just play with some friends when you feel like it."

The three of them were looking at me like I didn't understand field hockey. I could feel my face get hot, and my hands balled up. I stood up and faced them.

"I understand that I'm not going to be the star of the team. I understand that I might not even make the first line. But I can still be part of a team and still have fun," I snapped.

I looked at Dad. "And that is why you and Mom

tell us to play in the first place. So if I got that wrong, and you want me to be stressed out and beating myself up and not enjoying a morning on the field getting a great workout with some girls, let me know," I added.

Molly's and Jenna's eyes popped open wide. Even Dad looked like he didn't know what to say.

I looked at them all like they were crazy, grabbed a glass of water, and marched upstairs.

Maybe they could all go away, I thought, *and just leave me here in peace.*

Chapter Six

The More the Merrier—Not!

Monday mornings are the worst. The *worst*. But Monday mornings in my mind actually start on Sunday night.

Sunday night in our house is "planning night," according to Mom. We go over everyone's schedule for the week, and then Mom and Dad make sure everyone is covered—that means anyone who needs a ride or needs to be picked up somewhere has a parent to meet them or bring them where they need to be. Mom puts everything on the board, and some weeks can get pretty insane with all the scribbles.

Mom was just about to write in next weekend's plans when Jenna said, "It's Fall Fest this weekend!"

"Wow, that happened fast," said Mom. "Time is

just flying by." She shook her head and wrote it on the board.

Fall Fest is a big deal in town. One Saturday every fall, there is a festival with a parade, music, and food. The Park is a big part of it, and Donut Dreams, of course, because who doesn't love an apple cider donut at a fall festival?

A lot of the businesses or even school groups, like the high school field hockey team, have booths that sell stuff or give away things like T-shirts or even mugs. Everyone wears school colors, which are red and white.

That night, after performances from a few of the school choruses and the high school marching band, there's a big bonfire at the lake. Everyone comes down with blankets, and families sit together with chocolatey s'mores and watch the fireworks that end the night.

Fall Fest is also a big deal for our family. Since everyone in our family is usually a little crazy working at Fall Fest, between the food that the Park provides and the donuts that Donut Dreams sells in the morning, we have a tradition called Family Fall Fest.

So Jelly!

The night before, Dad fills in for Mom at the restaurant, helping to pack up food and equipment to move it to Main Street, which is where the parade and booths are.

Mom takes the three of us out for dinner—"just us girls," as we like to say—at one of our favorite restaurants, Louie Louie, which is a couple towns over. They have two things that we always get: fried ravioli and something called butter cake, which is this gooey vanilla cake that I could eat for days.

We actually get dressed up, even though the restaurant isn't too fancy, and it's a lot of fun. Even Molly wears a skirt or a dress.

"So next Friday is Family Fall Fest?" I asked excitedly.

"Seems that way," said Mom.

"Butter cake!" Molly yelled. "Yes! Oh, I can taste it already!"

"Fried ravioli!" cried Jenna.

"I want you to remember St. Louis fried ravioli the next time you think about going to school in California," teased Dad.

"I'll just have it when I come home, Dad!" said Jenna, laughing. "Besides, in California you can have strawberries all year round. Much healthier for you!"

"Yeah, but fried ravioli tastes better!" said Dad.

This perked me up. I loved Family Fall Fest, and I was excited because even if the week was a hard one—hello, math test—there was a really great weekend waiting for us.

"This year Lindsay is coming with us," said Mom.

She was acting as Dad's sous chef, chopping the veggies for the stir-fry he was making.

"To Fall Fest?" I asked, confused.

"No, to *Family* Fall Fest," said Mom without looking up. "I thought it would be nice to include her. The more the merrier."

"But Mom, it's supposed to be just US!" I wailed.

Mom looked up from the cutting board, surprised, and Dad turned around to look at me too.

I didn't mean to sound so angry about it, but a tradition was a tradition. It was pretty rare that the three sisters were together with just Mom, and besides, Family Fall Fest had always been that way.

"Well," said Mom slowly. "Lindsay is family. And Family Fall Fest is, well, about our family. I think she'd really appreciate being included."

"Well, if it's Family Fall Fest, then why not invite

Dad," I said testily. I knew it didn't sound very nice when I said it out loud, but I just couldn't help how angry I was.

"It's just girls," said Mom. "And Dad is helping Grandpa, Nans, Uncle Mike, and Uncle Charlie so they can prep for the next day." I could tell by her tone that she was quickly getting irritated and impatient with me.

"Kelsey, you have been such a brat all weekend," said Jenna. "What is going on?"

"I'm not a brat!" I yelled.

But even as I was saying it, deep down inside I knew I was.

"Girls!" said Dad. "Cease-fire!"

He and Mom exchanged glances, and I could tell that he had probably told her about how angry I got after being grilled about hockey practice.

"I've already invited her," said Mom in that kind of voice that means *this is done and we are not discussing it further.* "And she was so happy. Remember, Kelsey, that it's been a tough time for her, and family is all about being there for each other when times are tough."

"Well, it's been a tough year for me too!" I said,

and as Mom was opening her mouth, I added, "And no, I don't want to talk about it!"

I stomped up the stairs to my room, which thankfully was nice and quiet and, most importantly, away from my family.

In our house you can pretty much hear everyone from every room, and I could hear Mom and Dad murmuring about me and asking Molly what was going on at school.

A few minutes later there was a knock on my door, and, expecting it to be Mom or Dad telling me it was time for dinner, I said, "I'll be right there."

But Jenna poked her head in. "Hey, pip-squeak," she said, calling me a nickname that she hadn't used in a while.

She flopped down on the bed next to me and looked at my face. "Are you wearing lip gloss?"

I sighed. "Yeah."

"It looks nice," she said.

Then she ran out of the room and came back with what looked like a giant tube of lipstick.

"What's that?" I asked.

"A blush stick," she said. "Hold still."

She dotted the apples of my cheeks and rubbed

it in, then sat back and smiled. "Oh, that looks good. Go look."

I looked in the mirror on the back of my door. It looked like I had just gone for a brisk walk, and even though it wasn't obvious, I looked happier and a little glowy. But I did not feel glowy inside.

"Sometimes," said Jenna, "even when you don't feel great, you have to put on a happy face, and soon enough the rest of you follows."

"Huh?" I asked.

"Look, middle school is hard," said Jenna. "I get that. Your friends are changing and it seems like everything is happening all at once. But sometimes you just have to go with change and see where it takes you. It could be really good."

"So I should pretend to be happy all the time and just wear makeup to mask the grumpiness?" I asked.

"Not at all!" said Jenna. "That's not what I'm saying. You can be mad and sad and disappointed. But just saying no to trying something different and sitting out the chance to change isn't great either. You never know what new things could be exciting or open up new doors."

I moaned. "You sound like Mom," I complained.

"New opportunities! Well, what if I like the old opportunities?"

"I think you're missing the point," said Jenna. "Just be open. Just because Lindsay is coming with us to dinner doesn't mean that Family Fall Fest can't be great. It just means that while we're having one of our favorite nights, we're including someone who is family and who very much wants to be there with us. That's what family does, Kelsey."

I knew she was right, but she could be right and I could still be angry at the same time. I let those two things float around in my brain for a little bit.

"Dinner in five," said Jenna, and hopped up from the bed.

"Jenna?" I asked. "Will you miss us?"

"When?" she said.

"When you go to college in California. Will you miss us as much as we'll miss you?"

"Okay," said Jenna. "First of all, we still have a year and a half before I'm going anywhere. Second, I don't know for sure that I'm going to school in California. I have to be accepted first. And third of all," she said, holding up three fingers, "are you serious? I will miss you guys like crazy! I'll be thinking of the four of you and probably be lonely that it's just me on my own!"

"So why don't you just stay close?" I asked.

"I might," said Jenna. "But I also think it's kind of cool to see what I can do on my own. I'll always have my family, and it doesn't matter to me if they're five minutes or five hours away. I know they're there."

I thought about that. It mattered to me. I'd much rather be five minutes away from my family.

Jenna gave me a hug. "No matter where I am, I'm always your sister," she said. "Your big sister. Your big, bossy sister who will always tell you what to do, even when you're fifty!"

I giggled just as Molly appeared in the doorway. "What's so funny?" she said.

"Me when I'm fifty," I said.

"Huh?" said Molly. "Uh . . . okay. Dad sent me up to tell you it's dinnertime. It's the Sunday Special too. Shrimp."

Ugh, I hate shrimp.

See, sometimes Monday morning starts early.

Chapter Seven
Just Another Manic Monday

Principal Clarke was trying to get everyone's attention for the morning meeting. "It's a big week in Bellgrove!" she said. "Settle down and tune in, because there is a lot going on!"

I was sitting with our new crew, which was Isabella, Olivia, Hannah, Riley, Michelle, and Sophia. We filled out a whole table sitting together. *Addition is better than subtraction,* I heard Mom say in my head. I guess she should know; she is an accountant.

"First of all, the student council elections are coming up," said Principal Clarke. "This week you'll see those campaigns start with posters in the halls. Next week we'll hear from the candidates in prepared statements, and then we'll have a Q and A session, when you can ask them questions. Then we'll have the election. It's an exciting time at Bellgrove Middle School!"

I looked over at Hannah and Olivia. Olivia was biting her nails. I guess running for office could be stressful. There's no way I would ever want to sit in front of the entire school and answer questions. Ugh.

"Next," said the principal, "as many of you know, we have Fall Fest this weekend."

The room erupted in cheers.

She smiled. "I know, it's a great weekend. We have many opportunities to volunteer, so check the sign-up board in the back of the cafeteria if you'd like to help out. Even if you just come to the event, be sure to show your school spirit and wear your red and white colors!"

Sophia nudged me. "Can I borrow your red cardigan?" she asked. "The one with the pattern on it?"

I nodded.

The rest of the day was, well, it was a Monday. Somehow I smooshed my turkey sandwich that Dad packed me for lunch and the soup sloshed out from my thermos, soaking the brownie he'd put in there because we always got a special treat on Mondays.

I slammed my locker on my finger and was late to French class because I forgot my book and had to run back for it.

And because it was Family Fall Fest on Friday, we'd switched my day working at Donut Dreams to Monday for this week.

I trudged into the Park, and sure enough, Grandpa was waiting at the podium.

"Okay, this cranky face is getting to be familiar," he said. "And I don't like it."

I couldn't tell if he was teasing me or reprimanding me, so I tried to make my face look as happy as I could.

"It's been a Monday, Grandpa," I said.

"Mondays are rough," he said, nodding.

I don't know why, but just then I kind of flung myself at him and buried my head in his arm.

He gave me a big hug and patted my back. "Is this more than a miserable Monday?" he asked, concerned. "Everything okay, sweetie?"

My grandpa was what most people described as "a force," but he could also be a really big softy, especially with his grandchildren.

I took a big breath and lifted up my head. "Yeah," I said. "It's okay. Middle school is hard."

"Ahhh," he said. "Change is hard. Why do you think I just sit at this podium every day?" He chuckled and looked up as Mom was rounding the corner. "Melissa, your daughter says middle school is hard."

"What happened at school today?" asked Mom with a worried look.

"Nothing," I said.

Mom and Grandpa looked at each other, and Grandpa shrugged. "Well, something happened to your mom today," he said. "Big news!" He beamed.

Mom laughed. "Well, I don't know if it's big news, Dad. But they asked me to come speak at a conference in St. Louis about small businesses."

"It *is* big news!" said Grandpa. "Of all the people in that big city, they asked our Melissa! That's because she's so smart and such a good businessperson. She keeps this place humming!"

"Oh, just Melissa keeps this place running, huh, Dad?" teased Uncle Charlie as he put down his clipboard and came over to join us.

"When is the conference?" I asked, curious.

Mom never really went away on business trips, but once in a while she, Uncle Charlie, and Uncle Mike would go to a convention.

"It's in a few weeks, actually," said Mom. "Which means I need to put together a presentation pretty fast."

Uncle Mike came over then. "Is this a staff meeting?" he asked. "Or a family convention over here? Because I have donuts to sell and Fall Fest to plan. What does everyone think about red frosted donuts this year, so we're in with the school color theme?"

"Red donuts sound gross, Mike," Mom said. "Plus, they might not look too appetizing."

"Well, maybe more pink?" said Uncle Charlie. "Or you could just have jelly donuts. Those are red on the inside. And we're all red on the inside for Fall Fest!"

I laughed. "I'm reporting for duty," I said, saluting them and walking over to the donut counter.

Lindsay was there, as usual, before me. It should seem weird that she would beat me to work, since we both got out of school at the same time, but I took the bus home with Molly and then Dad or Jenna drove me over.

Lindsay was picked up at school by Nans, who brought her to the Park. I felt a little twinge just then because I got to go home, where Dad was always waiting for me.

After Lindsay's mom died, she came to the

restaurant with her dad after school. She and Skylar used to sit in a booth and do their homework until someone could take them home.

I remembered just then that Aunt Amy made these really great pies in the fall, and I wondered if Lindsay missed going home to her mom, in a kitchen that smelled like fresh apple pie.

Lindsay was helping Mrs. Ellis pack up a box of donuts to take to the soccer team.

"Hi, Mrs. Ellis," I said. "Mind if we put one in there for Molly?"

"Oh, this is for everyone on the team!" she said. "Or everyone trying out. Gosh, I hope they all make it. They are all such terrific girls."

I popped in a chocolate-glazed donut, which I knew was Molly's favorite. Then I threw in an old-fashioned donut, because I knew that was Riley's favorite. I didn't know what Isabella's favorite was.

"Okay, we have two of each kind," said Lindsay. "So hopefully no fights over who gets what!"

"Thanks, girls," said Mrs. Ellis.

After Mrs. Ellis there was a steady stream of customers picking up treats for after school or after practice.

"Welcome to Donut Dreams," I said, spinning around, ready to help the next customer.

I looked up and Ms. Castro, the town librarian, was smiling at me. "Hello, dear!" she said. "I was hoping you'd be here!"

"I'm usually here on Fridays and Sundays," I said. "But we had to change the schedule this week due to Fall Fest."

"Well, I haven't seen much of you since school started," she said. "I know the start of the year can be stressful, and I'm hoping you still have some time to stop by."

"You usually have trouble keeping me away!" I said. "I've been a little busy, but I've been meaning to come in. I heard about a book by P. J. Night that I really want to read."

"Oh, I know just the one you are talking about!" said Ms. Castro. "I'll put it on the reserve shelf for you!"

"Thank you!" I said.

I had been telling Ms. Castro that I wanted to do her job ever since I was really little and Dad would take me there for the story-time hour.

Dad and Mom would smile when I said I wanted to be the Bellgrove librarian and say, *We'll see. You can be anything, so let's see what you really love.* But I loved books and I loved to read. And I loved that library. I didn't see why I would have to look any further.

I packed up Ms. Castro's order and we finally had a break.

"Hi, there," Lindsay said. "Whew, that was a rush."

"Yeah," I said. "I guess busy is better than not."

"True," she said.

Then I remembered I had field hockey after work today. "This is such a long Monday," I moaned.

"Since when is there a short Monday?" asked Lindsay. "I'm starving. Nans forgot to pack me a snack. Want a donut?"

I shook my head no. "It's slow now. Go ahead and just sneak it," I said. "I'll be lookout."

Lindsay looked around, then pinched a jelly donut from the case. She bit into it.

"Mmm, these are so good," she said. "Want a bite?"

I nodded and leaned over, but when I bit into the donut, I must have hit a pocket of jelly, because it spurted out and a big blob landed on my nose.

"Ugh!" I said.

You never knew what was going to hit you in the face on a Monday.

Chapter Eight
I'm a Lot Like Dad

My Monday continued at field hockey practice. It was a really nice evening and after the day I'd had, I didn't mind having a chance to run with the fall air filling my lungs.

But every time I started to relax, Amanda would yell, "Pass, pass, pass," or "Downfield, faster!" She was barking orders at me and it really annoyed me.

Coach Wickstead called us over. "Okay, girls, I've seen some tremendous talent and some good hustle. This year we're going to have a starting team and what I'm calling the supporting team. If you're on the starting team, that means you start all games. The supporting team will sub in and rotate as I feel is right for each game."

Naturally, Amanda made the starting team. So did Sophia! Isabella, Olivia, and I were part of the supporting team, which was okay with me.

I gave Sophia a big hug. "Hey, A-lister!" I said.

"Are you disappointed?" she asked.

"I'm kind of relieved," I said. "I like the game, but I'm not sure I like the pressure."

"I get that," said Sophia. "And we still get to practice together! But that one makes me nervous."

She motioned toward Amanda.

Amanda came over. "Congratulations, Sophia," she said. "Kelsey, you're a good player. You gave me a run for my money during some of those drills!"

I was surprised, but I couldn't help smiling. I gave Amanda a run for her money?

That night at dinner Mom told us about the conference she'd been asked to present at. It was all about how small businesses managed their finances and grew.

To be honest, it sounded a little boring, but it was still pretty cool to have a mom who spoke at conferences.

Dad raised his glass and said, "Let's all toast your awesome mother!"

Then he marked the weekend she'd be away on the calendar to "make it official."

For some of the trips Mom or Dad made to St. Louis, we took turns going with them. Molly had gone with Dad over the summer when he went for a certification course. Jenna went with Mom a few weeks ago for back-to-school shopping. So this meant it was my turn.

"Hey, I'm supposed to go with you to the city next!" I said. "Just the two of us."

"Well," said Mom, "I need to check the school calendar and see if it will work. Plus, this time I'm not just attending a conference. I have to speak there, so it might be different. But yes, you are up in the batting order."

I was excited. A trip with Mom would be lots of fun, and I couldn't even remember the last time it was just me with Mom. She'd be all mine. I was almost hopping up and down in my chair just thinking about it.

"How was everyone's day?" asked Dad. "Besides Big Shot Mom's?"

"Everyone is getting ready for Fall Fest," Jenna said. "The tennis team has a booth where we'll be doing face painting. It's going to be a lot of fun."

"The soccer team is working at the balloon booth. But no one knows how to make balloon animals," said Molly.

"Did you hear Mike's latest plan?" asked Mom. "He wants to do red donuts. Or at least jelly donuts, because they're red inside."

"Red donuts don't sound too great," said Dad, making a face.

"What about red velvet? Red velvet donuts could be very tasty," Mom said.

"Oh. Okay, I didn't think of that," Dad said. "I'm building a new stand for the Park this year that has a red awning. It's going to look fantastic."

"The field hockey team is helping the Park," I said.

"Ooh, that's great!" said Mom. "We could use the help."

"Yep, that was my idea," I said. "We can help serve."

"So when will they announce the final team?" asked Dad.

"Oh, they already did!" I said. "I made the supporting team, but not the starting team."

Everyone looked up.

"Good job, Kels!" said Jenna.

"Way to go!" said Molly.

"Why didn't you tell us?" asked Mom.

"It's not really a big deal," I said. "As I predicted, because there were only four girls from my grade, we all made it. I'm not playing on the A team, but it's okay. I still get to practice, and maybe next year I'll start."

Dad nodded. "That's right. You can play and have fun and see if you want to play more competitively next year."

"Do you think Riley will make the soccer team?" I asked Molly.

Molly nodded. "She's really good. I'm not sure about Isabella, though. She hasn't played as much."

Ha ha, I thought, then stopped myself because I wasn't sure exactly why I wouldn't want Isabella to make the team. I wondered how Riley would feel playing alone.

Later that night I was finishing homework and Dad came into my room, holding a piece of paper.

"Hi, Kelsey," he said. "So I have the hockey schedule, and I marked the games I think I can make."

"Oh," I said. "Dad, I don't think I'll even be playing."

"Well, that's okay," he said. "You're still part of the team, right?"

"Yeah," I said. "And it turns out I like being part of a team. It's fun. But I don't love the pressure of game day. I get too stressed out."

"That's how I was!" said Dad.

"You were?" I asked, surprised.

"Yep. When I played soccer, I loved the game, but I hated game day. I was always too nervous that I'd do something stupid and everyone would be there watching me."

"So what did you do?" I asked.

"Well, I realized it really was about being a good teammate and just playing my best," said Dad. "Winning or losing didn't change the game for me, and that was always my mantra."

"That sounds fun," I said. "And not complicated. Like just show up and have fun and don't worry about standings or playoffs or stats."

"Exactly," said Dad. "Even when people around you are getting a little crazy or excited, you just need to remember to listen to your own voice and stay centered. Even if someone is yelling that you made a dumb play, you just act like you have a colander in your brain."

"A colander in my brain?" I asked.

"Yes," said Dad. "A colander, like the kind we use when we drain the pasta water in the sink. But a colander in your brain means that you hear the good stuff and the positive stuff and you drain out all the bad stuff."

"Well, sometimes it's important to hear bad stuff," I said, thinking about how Mom would tell us that we had to be called out on our bad behavior so we'd recognize it.

"Of course," said Dad. "Constructive criticism is great and it can be very useful. But I'm talking about how nuts people can get in the heat of a game. That kind of stuff you just need to let go."

I nodded. I sort of understood.

"You know, Kelsey, if you don't want to play at all you don't have to, but once the season starts, you need to commit. So as of tomorrow you're in or out."

"I know," I said. I also knew that Dad was giving me a way out. I could just come home after school and not play on the team and not even have to worry about Amanda. Was that what I wanted?

All of a sudden, I was really tired.

"You know what I think you need?" asked Dad. "A good night's sleep."

"Yeah," I said, yawning. "And you know what else I really need? I really need Monday to be over."

I hoped that when I went to bed later, I wouldn't just lie there thinking about everything. Tonight, more than anything, I needed a deep, dreamless sleep. And a fresh start in the morning.

Chapter Nine
Team Spirit At Last

Olivia was waving to me at the lunch table, and I groaned a little inside because I really just wanted to hang with Sophia, Michelle, and Riley so I could talk to them about my hockey doubts.

"Addition is better than subtraction," I repeated to myself.

"Hello, teammate!" Olivia chirped.

"Hi, B squad teammate!" I said.

She laughed. "Go B team, go B team! Hey, here's another B-lister!" she said as Hannah sat next to Olivia, setting her tray down carefully so she didn't spill her chili.

"Hey, I can live with B-list hockey, but I hope I'll be in A-list student council," Hannah said. "We have so much work to do. I also have a lot of ideas."

"Can I help?" asked Isabella, as she sat down and spread out her lunch.

"Sure!" said Olivia. "But I thought you thought it was a dumb idea to run for student council."

Hmm, I thought. *So maybe that's why Olivia and Isabella weren't BFFs anymore. Because Olivia decided to run for student council with Hannah?*

"I didn't say it was a dumb idea," said Isabella. "I said I wasn't as interested in it. And that's okay. We can do different things and still be friends. Plus, I said I'd help you with your campaign."

"Well, it hurt my feelings," said Olivia.

"Olivia, I'm just not a student council person," said Isabella. "I don't have the patience to listen to people, and getting up in front of the school and speaking . . . ugh."

I was surprised. Isabella was an outgoing person. "I get that," I said.

"Right?" said Isabella, turning to me. "Can you imagine getting up at that podium?" She shivered.

"It's not a big deal," said Olivia. "We've known all these people for years!"

"It's totes a big deal," said Isabella. "Trust me."

"Okay," said Olivia. "Then if you don't mind and you still want to, I need help. We need a whole strategy and a plan for what we want the council to act on in the next year."

Isabella took out her phone. "Of course I want to help. That's what friends do. I've got my list maker here. Let's start."

Sophia sat down. "The line in the cafeteria is so long and so slow that now I have about three seconds to eat lunch!" she said.

"Well, there's one," said Olivia. "Make the cafeteria more efficient."

"Or give students a longer lunch period," said Michelle as she wheeled over next to me.

"Oh, that's a good one," said Olivia.

Sophia turned to me. "You can work with student council when you become our class representative," she said.

"I'm not even sure what the class rep does," I said.

"You heard Principal Clarke," said Isabella. "You represent us and talk through what our concerns are so that the council and teachers have some input. And the people who are in charge of making decisions will hear our voices and keep us informed about what's going on. This way, if we request something, and if we can't have it, hopefully we won't just hear a flat no. We will hear the reason behind it. We'll be able to keep our fellow classmates informed about everything going on."

"But that's not me," I said. "I have no idea how most people feel about things."

"But you are sensitive and a good listener," said Michelle. "You always see the best in things. And you really get people. You know just what they need."

I wondered who she was talking about, because that sure didn't seem like me lately. Lately I felt grouchy and selfish.

"Not so sure about that, Michelle," I said. I looked around. "Hey, where's Riley?"

Nobody knew, which was odd.

"Maybe she decided to study in the library," said Isabella. "We have a coding test next period."

We all hurried to finish our lunch.

"Write that down," said Sophia to Olivia. "Stop rushing us through the day. I don't deal well with rushing!"

Olivia nodded. "I can try, but I can't invent more hours in the day. That's a little beyond me!"

We laughed as the bell rang.

"And that's a wrap!" said Isabella.

"Ugh!" said Sophia, shoving a mini burrito in her mouth. "I'm definitely going to get a stomachache."

As I was headed out, I saw Riley in the hall, and she didn't look great.

"What's wrong?" I asked.

"Get a pass and meet me in the bathroom!" she whispered.

So I asked for a restroom pass and met her there. "What's up?" I asked, checking the stalls to see if anyone else was in there.

"I don't want to play in the soccer scrimmage today," said Riley.

"What? Why?"

"Because I'm scared," said Riley. "It's super competitive. Your sister and the other girls have been playing for a while, and it's my first year. What if I make a stupid play, or fall on my face?"

"You won't!" I said.

Riley looked at me.

"Okay, even if you do, what's the worst that can happen?" I asked.

"People will laugh?" said Riley.

"Well, then they aren't good teammates," I said. "Look, you made the team! That means you're a good player!"

"If I mess up everyone will wonder why I made the team," she said.

"Or they'll just think you had a rough day on the field, but that you tried, which is the most important thing," I said.

"What if I lose the game for the whole team?" she asked.

"One person can never lose a game for a team. It takes a whole team to win or lose a game," I replied.

Riley stared at me for a moment. "Okay, since when did you become Tammy Teammate and what have you done with Kelsey?" she asked.

"Well, I'm trying to help you," I said. "Besides, you just need to block everyone out during the game. You are a good player and you love the game. Just keep thinking about that and don't listen to the voice that says you can't do it."

"Thanks," said Riley. "And I'm glad you aren't mad at me."

"Why would I be mad at you?" I said.

"I thought you'd just be mad that I didn't play

hockey with you and Soph because we do almost everything together," she said.

"I'm disappointed we can't all play together," I said. "But I want you to do what you love and what you're good at. And we don't always have to do everything together to stay friends."

Huh, I thought. *That's kind of like what Isabella said to Olivia.* And it made a lot of sense.

"We are still friends, right?" Riley said.

"What?" I said. "Of course!"

"Well, I figured you and Sophia were so mad that I kind of got kicked out of the peas in a pod club. I like Isabella a lot, but it's not the same as the four of us."

"You can't get kicked out of this club," I said firmly.

"We probably are going to get kicked out of class if we don't get back there," said Riley.

She splashed some water on her face.

"Better?" I asked.

She nodded. "Thanks, Kels," she said. "You always know exactly what to say to make me feel better."

"That's what friends are for!" I said as I pushed open the bathroom door.

"Even when they throw up from nerves on the soccer field?" she said.

"Even then," I said. "But try not to do that. You'll be the Wetsy Betsy of the soccer team."

"Oh no," said Riley, stifling a laugh. "I'll be Ralphing Riley! I'll be known forever as the girl who spewed her lunch on the goal line!"

We were both laughing hard as we scurried back to class, but my conversation with Riley got me thinking.

I hadn't wet my pants in school or thrown up on a field. I likely wouldn't be the star of the hockey team. So what would I be known as?

Chapter Ten
Everything's Going Wrong

That afternoon Sophia and I decided to go along with Dad to Molly and Riley's soccer game for support.

"Do me a favor," I said to Molly. "Look out for Riley, because she's really nervous."

"Well, that's normal. I still get nervous before games," said Molly.

I was surprised. "You do?"

"Sure," said Molly. "What if I make a stupid play in front of everyone?"

"That's what she's worried about!" I said.

Sophia and I sat on the bleachers with Dad and cheered on the team. They were really good, especially Riley. She was running up and down the field super fast.

"It's like watching lightning!" Dad said.

The team won, and I was really happy watching Riley jump up and down at the end of the game. Sophia and I ran down for hugs.

"See, no Ralphing Riley!" I said.

"Thank goodness!" said Riley. "Molly really helped me out. She's a good teammate."

I smiled and reminded myself to thank Molly for that later.

"You can make it up to me by watching me sit on the bench during our hockey game!" I suggested.

Sophia rolled her eyes. "Just because you don't start doesn't mean you won't play!" she said.

"Oh, I hope I don't play!" I laughed. "I don't need that stress!"

But the next day it was me on the field for another scrimmage game, and I looked up to see Dad and Molly in the stands with Riley. I felt embarrassed because they really were watching me just sit there.

The game was a tough one, and I was cheering on Sophia, who was defending against a really aggressive player from the other team. I flinched a few times, but she hung in there.

The sun was sinking and it was getting a little

chilly, especially since I was only warming the bench and not myself.

There were only a few minutes left in the game when Coach Wickstead blew her whistle for a time-out. "Okay, the front line is tired. Time to start subbing in, girls."

I wasn't really paying attention, which was probably why I missed that she called my name.

"Are you sure?" I asked, as she motioned to me.

"You're up, Kelsey," she said. "Let's see what you can do."

I felt sick to my stomach.

Sophia was playing next to me, and she jogged over. "Okay, Kelsey. You can do this. Play like we're not playing a game. Play like we're just out here on the field, having a good time. Ignore everything else."

I nodded. I remembered what Dad told me. *A colander in your brain means that you hear the good stuff and the positive stuff and you drain out all the bad stuff.*

Colander, I thought. *Use a colander.*

The ball dropped and off we went. I took Sophia's advice and decided to just pretend we were practicing. I used Dad's advice and blocked out the other girls.

I'm actually holding my own, I thought.

So Jelly!

I vaguely heard Dad yelling, "Go, Kelsey, go!" and Riley yelling, "You got it, Kelsey!" but I just tried to shut everything out.

In the huddle, Amanda said, "You're doing great, Kelsey. I'm going to pass to Sophia, and she'll pass to Tracey, who'll pass the ball back to me, and then I'll pass to you. I need you to be close to the crease to get the ball in. Okay?"

"Okay," I said.

It felt like the whole play was in slow motion. Amanda set the play up as she said. She passed to Sophia, who passed to Tracey, who was running fast up the field. Amanda ran into place and passed the ball to me.

It was a clear shot and I was concentrating on not missing. I pivoted and *thwack*, hit the ball. I watched it arc and hit the post . . . and bounce out.

I stood there for a second, stunned. It was a shot I had made a million times before.

In the second I paused, the other team scooped up the ball and trampled down toward their goal. I heard them yelling in victory as I stood there, alone, near our goalkeeper.

I had just lost the game.

I felt like I couldn't move. I saw Dad stand up and look at me, while Molly covered her eyes with her hands.

It was Sophia who came jogging back up the field and put her arm around me.

"Great shot!" she said. "It was a great shot and you got it up the field."

We walked back to the bench, my head hanging low. I didn't want to talk to anyone.

"Good game, girls," Coach Wickstead was saying. "Nice hustle out there and great teamwork. Good to see you on the field, Kelsey. Next time we're going to have you play longer."

Longer? Was she crazy? How would that help?

Everyone gathered their things, and I took my backpack and walked toward Dad.

"Great game!" he said cheerily, and I gave him a sour look.

"You can't make every shot you take!" said Molly encouragingly. "You looked good out there!"

Riley gave me a hug and whispered, "You did good and you didn't throw up!"

"Can we just go home?" I asked.

On the way home I got a text from Michelle.

So Jelly!

> **Hey u! Sorry I missed the game today. How was field hockey?**

I sighed. I really wasn't in the mood to rehash the game right now. I texted back,

> **It was OK, TTYL.**

At home we had a quick dinner and we all settled in for homework. I don't know how Jenna plays music while she does homework; I need total quiet.

I was startled when there was a knock at my door. Mom poked her head in.

"I had an idea," she said. "This conference I'm speaking at happens to be during fall break, so you have that Friday off school. What if I take you and Lindsay to St. Louis with me, and we can make it a little fun weekend trip?"

Suddenly I was furious. I didn't know if it was the tough week or I was more sore about the game than I'd thought, but I just sputtered, "Lindsay?"

"Yessss," said Mom slowly, walking into my room. "I thought it would be nice to include her. She might like a special trip out of town."

I crossed my arms over my chest. "Mom, you know who else would like a special trip out of town? With her mother? Just with her mother? Because her sisters each got a turn going by themselves and didn't have to share a parent?" I was kind of yelling.

"You don't think it would be nice to include Lindsay?" asked Mom, raising her voice just a little.

"It probably would!" I was actually yelling now. "But I don't want to! This is *my* trip. You are *my* mother. And it's *my* turn!"

"Okay, let's take a breath here," said Dad, who came into the room.

"I don't want to take a breath!" I said. "I'm so sick of tiptoeing around Lindsay! I'm sorry she's had a tough time. But my mother is here and I shouldn't have to give up my trip with my mother just because my mother isn't dead!"

Mom drew in her breath sharply. "Kelsey Jane Lakes!" she yelled.

From the other room, I heard Molly say to Jenna, "I can't believe she just said that."

For some reason that made me even madder. I felt like my two sisters were teaming up against me! Mom and Dad were also looking at me like they didn't know who I was or what to say to me.

"Time-out here," said Dad. "Kelsey, I don't think you meant what just came out. I know you didn't. But we're all a little worked up here, so let's take a breath and calm down before we say anything else we might regret."

Mom and Dad shut the door behind them.

I threw myself down on my bed. I don't know why I was so moody and so angry lately. It was just that so much was happening and so much was changing, and nobody seemed to understand what I was feeling. I didn't even know what I was feeling half the time.

All I wanted to do was make everything go back to the way it was.

I opened up my notebook and tried to do some math homework, but it was hard to concentrate. After a while I just pushed the book away and stretched out on my bed, staring up at the ceiling.

Then I got up and put my pajamas on. I wanted to go to bed early and forget this horrible day ever happened.

About an hour later Dad knocked on my door. "How about some cookies and milk?" he asked.

I nodded and followed him down to the kitchen.

I saw the light was on in Mom's office, so I guessed she was working on her presentation.

Dad had made chocolate chip cookies, which were my favorite. They were still warm from the oven, and I washed the first few bites down with some cold milk. I was still annoyed, but the warm cookies were helping.

"Doesn't get any better than that, does it?" Dad said, grinning.

I swallowed and waited. I was sure I was going to get a speech or something.

"We can see that things are a little topsy-turvy this year," said Dad. "You have a lot going on."

I waited.

"Your friends are all trying new things, like different sports or student council."

I guessed Molly had told them about Hannah and Olivia.

"And I get that getting into the groove at work is difficult as well. And we expect a lot of you between school and holding down a job, when not many of your other friends work."

I nodded.

"If school and Donut Dreams are too much, we

can dial back the number of days you work," said Dad. "Maybe two days is just too much right now."

I shrugged.

"Now as for your cousin Lindsay," he said.

I stared down at my lap. I knew I wasn't being kind about Lindsay.

"I know you and Lindsay are close," Dad said. "And I know you care about her. You really looked out for her when her mom first passed away a couple years ago. And I know that can sometimes feel like a burden."

"It's not a burden," I said.

"No, it is," said Dad. "It's still a burden even if you're happy to do it. It means that you're shouldering caring for someone else, and doing that takes up a lot of energy."

"I'm different," I blurted out.

Dad was about to say something, then stopped. "Different how?"

"I'm not competitive. I like living in this small town. I don't want to go away to college. I don't want to run for student council. And I don't want to share Mom with anyone more than Jenna and Molly, because sharing her with them is already too much.

And I don't know why everyone wants me to be the class representative."

Whoa. That all just came out.

"Okay," said Dad, and I could see that this was maybe more than he thought he'd get into. He rubbed his head.

"First of all, there's nothing wrong with not being competitive. And you're right, your personality is way different from your sisters', and that's okay. As for not moving away, well, your mother and I grew up here, so no arguments on that front." He thought for a second.

"And about sharing Mom, well, we know that's a lot to ask. You're right about that. You, Jenna, and Molly all need your mother. And she tries really hard to make sure you all get what you need from her. But right now Lindsay needs her too. You may not think that's fair, but sometimes what's needed outweighs fair. Yes, the family is worried about Lindsay, and about Sky. But I can tell you that after your performance the past week, we're all pretty worried about you, too."

Good, I thought.

"You've always been the happy-go-lucky one," Dad said. "But this past week you've been sad and moody, sometimes for no reason. Or at least no reason that's obvious to the rest of us."

He paused as if he was waiting for me to say something. But I didn't feel like discussing the bad mood I'd been in all week.

"So is Lindsay coming to St. Louis?" I asked.

"I'm not sure," said Dad. "Mom and I need to talk about it."

"Okay," I said. "Can I go back upstairs now?"

Dad gave a big sigh, like he was relieved. "Sure. Actually, that's a good idea. Why don't we all get a good night's sleep and talk about it when we're fresh tomorrow?"

As I went back upstairs, I passed Mom's office. I heard her clicking away at her keyboard and I stopped for a second, hoping she would open the door, but she didn't.

I felt guilty about yelling at her and guilty that I had a mother I fought with.

I went up the stairs and saw Jenna's door was open. Jenna and I have always been super close. Mom and Dad loved to tell me the story of when they brought me home from the hospital and Jenna yelled, "MY baby! MY Kelsey!" and told everybody I was *her* baby, and she would try to hold me and feed me any chance she could get.

Jenna was in bed with her laptop, doing homework, and I crawled in next to her. When I was really little, I would scoot across the hall and get into bed with Jenna when I was scared.

Tonight, Jenna didn't even blink. She pulled up the covers around me without saying a word and I snuggled in. I could smell her shampoo on her pillow, which always reminded me of roses.

If I closed my eyes, maybe the week would be over faster, and we could all just start again.

Chapter Eleven
A Good Talk

Luckily, the rest of the week was kind of quiet. Mom and Dad didn't mention St. Louis, and I knew well enough not to bring it up.

On Thursday, I had another hockey game, and I was a little nervous about being thrown in. After some really nice fall weather it had been warm again, and the late afternoon sun felt like it was burning me as I sat on the hot metal bleacher.

I noticed that Dad had shown up at my game again. He never waved at me or anything, but I saw him sitting there with his hands crossed over his long legs. Most of the parents were on their phones or chatting, but he was always sitting off a little bit, just watching.

It was nice to know that even for that short period of time, I had his full attention.

Sure enough, Coach Wickstead blew her whistle and called, "Kelsey, let's go. You're in!"

I took a deep breath, smiled at the thumbs-up from Sophia, who was coming off the field for a break, and ran to my spot.

I took my cues from Amanda and Tracey, and I ran down the field with the ball. I passed to Tracey, who broke free and scored. We all cheered, and I was happy as I ran off the field.

Somehow when I jumped up to play I'd lost my water bottle, and I had to go search for it under the bench. When I came back, Dad had made his way down the stands and was talking to Coach Wickstead.

Coach had gone to school with my uncle Mike and had known Dad for a long time too. They were talking about the game when I came trotting up.

"Nice playing today, Kelsey," Coach said.

"Thank you," I said. "I think those six minutes were really important!" Then I laughed.

"Hey, six minutes can win or lose a game," said Coach. "Every player adds something."

I tried hard not to laugh again, because I didn't

think I was anywhere close to being an anchor for the team.

"You know why I love watching her play?" Coach asked Dad.

"Because she's good!" Dad said, and I could tell from his voice that he really meant it.

"Well, yes, she is," said Coach. She looked at me. "I love watching you play because I can tell you love it. I love watching a player smile as she races across the grass with her hair flying out and the wind behind her. It does my coach and my player heart good."

I was surprised.

"We have a lot of talent on the team," Coach continued, "and each player really brings something unique. Some bring skill, some bring a competitive spirit, some are just workhorses. But you, Kelsey, you are rare." She tilted her head at me. "You remind everyone on that field that this is fun, that this can be exhilarating. Any good team needs that."

Dad was smiling really widely. "I always tell her that it's not about winning or losing," he said.

"It isn't!" said Coach. "It's about the joy of the game. And you definitely show us how that works."

I looked at her to see if she was buttering me up

or something. I mean, it sounded like something Dad or Mom would say to me to make me feel better, but a coach?

"Kelsey, you remind me of me when I used to play for fun," said Coach. "I know you don't love competing, but I think if we can get you more comfortable, then you can play longer and longer and the competition of the game won't faze you. By next year I'll have you playing full halves. And you'll still be loving the game. That's my goal for you."

"Well," I said. "I guess I can work on that."

"We can work on your skills," said Coach. "But I don't want you to work the fun out of your game. I want you to enjoy it. I want you relaxed. I want you to always have a blast. Does that make sense?"

I nodded. It did. "But isn't it *also* about winning the game?"

Coach laughed. "Well, if we were selling tickets in a big stadium and I had to win all the time, maybe I'd feel differently. But I'm more interested in showing a great team how wonderful this sport can be."

Dad reached over and put his arm around me.

"You're doing right by this one, Chris," Coach Wickstead said.

"Don't I know it!" Dad said. "Now we have to do right by her history teacher by getting her homework done!"

We waved to Coach as we headed off the field.

Dad and I were quiet, walking to the car, and we drove in silence. But before we got back through town, Dad pulled into the Frosty Freeze parking lot.

"What are you doing?" I asked.

He looked a little guilty. "You had a good game. It's just a little celebration that's not a donut!"

"You don't have to ask me twice," I said, and shot out of the car.

We walked up to the window and I ordered a King Frosty, which was a big milkshake with tons of ice cream, whipped cream, and butterscotch syrup.

"If I eat this whole thing, I'm probably not going to do too well on dinner," I said.

"Well, it's Mom's turn to make dinner tonight," said Dad. "So . . ."

"Dad!" I said, but I laughed. Mom was a terrible cook.

Dad ordered a King Frosty with chocolate sauce, and we headed toward the picnic tables to slurp them down.

"We have to hide the evidence and get rid of the cups before we get in the car," Dad said.

I was slurping away when Dad said, "So, like I said the other night, we're a little worried about you, Kelsey."

"I remember you said you were worried the other night," I said. "But why?"

"Because usually you don't let things bother you. You live by your own rules at your own pace. Mom and I have always marveled about that. You don't need to go off to a big city to prove anything; you'll be just as happy moving twenty feet away. You know yourself, and you're confident. And that's special."

Huh. Here I'd been thinking that was just boring, not special.

"But lately you seem the opposite of happy. I don't know if it's a phase or an adjustment or if there's something going on, but I want to remind you we are here to talk and help."

I took a big slurp and thought about it. I wanted to talk to Dad, but even I wasn't too sure why things were bothering me so much.

"I don't do too well with change," I said slowly.

Dad nodded and waited for me to go on.

"Sometimes I have all these feelings that come at

once, and I don't know where they're coming from or why I feel them. And when that happens, I just want everything to go back to the way it was."

"I get that," said Dad. "In a lot of ways Mom and I always want the three of you to be really little again, when a lollipop could solve any drama and make everything better. It was easier."

"Are you trying to tell me this is hard for everyone involved?" I said, kind of teasing him.

"Yes!" said Dad. "Because sometimes I don't know what I'm doing and I'm just making it up as I go."

"Dad!" I yelped. "You're the dad! You're supposed to know exactly what to say and what to do!"

"Doesn't work that way," said Dad. "There's no manual. Mom and I figure it out as we go. Sometimes we don't get it right. We should have seen that Mom spending a lot of time with Lindsay could make you feel a little neglected."

I looked down. "I feel bad about that," I said, using my toe to dig in the sand under the table.

"Well, we'd like you to see that Lindsay needs all of us. But it's also a really natural way to feel, and we get that, too. Mom feels terrible."

"She does?"

"Yep, she feels like she's letting you all down by spreading herself too thin."

Poor Mom. I knew she was trying. Now I felt extra bad.

"So it's okay that I feel bad about Lindsay and want to help her but still feel mad that she gets Mom's attention when I need it too?"

"Of course!" said Dad. "That's totally normal. We just should have seen it coming and been able to help work through that stuff."

"So how do we make this better?"

"I haven't read that far in the manual yet," said Dad, smiling. "But don't worry, I'm getting to that chapter next."

I laughed and chucked the cup in the trash.

Dad stood up and made a hoop shot into the can.

"Nice!" I said, and we jumped back into the car.

We hadn't solved anything, but I felt so much better. It was amazing what a good game, a good shake, a good talk, and a great dad could do.

Chapter Twelve
Clearing the Air

Poor Principal Clarke could barely get us to settle down for announcements on Friday. Everyone was buzzing about Fall Fest.

"Attention! Attention!" she kept saying.

Finally, she nodded to Mr. Schmitt, the lacrosse coach, who blew his whistle so loudly that everyone covered their ears, but it did the trick.

"I know we're all excited about Fall Fest," Principal Clarke said, "but we have a whole day of school to get through before the weekend kicks in!"

She surveyed the room. "Okay, now a quick announcement before we start the day. I have the results of our class representative election. Well, it wasn't really an election, it was more of a nomination.

The students who received the most nominations for each class will serve as class rep for one year. Now, for our sixth-grade students, the rep will be Kelsey Lakes."

Sophia, Riley, and Michelle were hugging me, and everyone at my table was yelling, "Whoo-hoo," so loudly that I didn't even hear the names of the reps for the other classes.

"If the reps I just announced can meet me during their lunch periods today, we can talk more about these exciting new responsibilities."

The bell rang and everyone flooded out into the hall, talking and laughing.

Lindsay gave me a hug. "Ms. Rep!" she said.

"I knew you'd win!" Michelle said.

Molly pulled on my ponytail. "Hey, sis, you won't forget about the little people who know all your family secrets now that you're an elected official, right? You'd better be nice to me."

It was exciting, but I had no idea what I had just gotten myself into. Or more specifically, what my class had just got me into . . .

I knocked on Principal Clarke's door at lunch, and she called, "Come in."

So Jelly!

I peeked my head in and she said, "Oh, Kelsey, welcome! Come on in!"

She moved over some piles of papers on her desk and motioned for me to sit down. "Did you bring your lunch? Oh good, we can eat together."

I unscrewed my thermos and wondered if it was okay to eat ravioli in front of my principal.

She brought over a thermos of soup and sat down and started talking, so I just decided to shovel in my lunch while I had the chance.

"I'm so excited for you to be in this position, Kelsey," she said. "And I can't say I'm surprised that your classmates nominated you, as I think you're the perfect person for this job."

"Um, exactly what is this job?" I asked.

I was panicking a little at the word "job." I already had a job, and one was quite enough, but two? Ugh.

"Well, it's mostly about being the person who students can come to with their issues or concerns. This is a new position, so we're just feeling it out right now, but our hope is that one day per month we'd be able to set you up in an office or at a desk," she said. "Your classmates can come talk to you about things like changing the lunch menu or getting more involved with the volunteer safety team in town, that kind of thing."

I nodded. "Maybe there could also be an e-mail address for this role, so if someone doesn't want to wait, they can always contact me," I said.

"Oh, that's a great idea!" Principal Clarke beamed at me. "I knew you'd be good at this!"

"Okay, but . . . ," I said. "Well, what am I supposed to do with these issues?"

I panicked a little more. Was I supposed to solve these problems? I could barely solve my own problems!

"You'd bring them to a monthly committee meeting we'd have with all three of the class reps, me, and a few teachers who have volunteered to help. We'll talk through what's possible, like maybe offering a more diverse lunch menu, and what's not, like the suggestion I think you'll get to shorten the school day!"

"Okay," I said. "So it's basically a listening position?"

"Exactly," said Principal Clarke. "I think students feel better when they know there's an ear listening to them. Most people do. You aren't expected to solve any issues and you won't be making major changes, but you'll be a sympathetic voice and you'll be able to help them voice their concerns to us. I truly believe that a lot of frustration comes when people think they aren't being heard."

The bell rang.

"Oh my, these lunch periods do go by quickly, don't they?" Principal Clarke said as she gulped her soup.

"My friends and I were just talking about that!" I said. "Students really need more time to eat!"

"So do teachers and principals!" said Principal Clarke. "Great point. Let's put that on the list! Can't wait to get started!"

As I walked to my next class, I thought about my new job. I would have to listen to my classmates' concerns and suggestions, and then Principal Clarke would listen to me and the other class reps. Then Principal Clarke and the other teachers would try to figure something out.

First, Dad didn't know how to figure out how to solve my issues. Now Principal Clarke admitted she wasn't sure how to solve whatever might come up.

One thing was for sure: I was surrounded by

adults who really needed to start giving me answers.

※　※　※　※　※

On Friday afternoon Jenna, Molly, and I were squeezing each other in and out of the bathroom as we showered and dried our hair.

The doorbell rang and I knew it was probably Lindsay.

"Can you get the door?" Jenna yelled.

I went downstairs because I was the only one who was dressed. I was wearing a pink-and-gray minidress and short gray boots.

Jenna was doing our hair and helping us pick out outfits, and she was arguing with Molly about whether pink and orange actually went together.

Lindsay was standing on the front step, and I waved to Nans backing out of the driveway.

"Welcome to chaos," I said. "The fashion team is upstairs."

Lindsay followed me into Jenna's room, where it looked like she had every outfit she owned on the floor.

"Hey, Linds," said Jenna. "Do you need a fashion consult or are you all set?"

"Uh," said Lindsay, looking down. "You tell me?"

Jenna took a moment to take in Lindsay's outfit. "You look great," Jenna said, and she really did.

Lindsay had her shiny hair in waves and she had on this really cute blue denim dress that tied at the waist, and boots.

"Did your grandmother get that for you?" Jenna asked.

"Uh-huh," said Lindsay.

Her mom's mom lived in Chicago and was always sending her these great outfits that she'd found.

I was a little jealous because the shopping is not great out here. Everyone always dresses the same because everyone ends up at the same stores, or ordering online, which is kind of annoying.

Lindsay turned to me and smiled shyly. "You look nice, Kels," she said.

I just nodded and sort of grunted at her. I still wasn't exactly thrilled that she was coming with us.

Lindsay seemed to pick up on my grumpy attitude. "You okay?" she said.

"I'm fine," I lied. "Just looking for my gray bag," which was practically right in front of me. "Oh, here it is."

I grabbed it and walked away from Lindsay as quickly as I could. I glanced back for a moment and saw her watching me with a puzzled look on her face.

"Are you girls ready?" Mom called from down the hall.

She was running late because things at the Park were always crazy the day before Fall Fest. The Park provides almost all the food, so there's a ton of setup and prep work. When she called us, she already sounded a little frazzled.

"Mom, you're going to shower, aren't you?" Jenna asked. She looked worried.

"Yes," said Mom. "Don't worry, I won't embarrass you, Jenna!"

Mom can get ready faster than anyone I know. Sometimes when she and Dad go out we time her, and she can take a shower, get dressed, and do her hair and makeup in twelve minutes flat.

"I don't have extra time, so I get used to doing things fast!" she says.

Since Jenna knew Mom would be ready soon, she hustled into an outfit and gave up arguing with Molly, whom I thought looked really cute in an orange dress with a pink jean jacket over it.

Within fifteen minutes, we were all in the car and headed to Louie Louie. Mom had the radio on and we were all singing along. I kept looking at Lindsay to see if she felt out of place, but she seemed like she was happy to be there.

Mrs. Selden has been the owner of Louie Louie forever, and she gave us all hugs when she saw us. "Now, let's see how beautiful everyone is getting. Oh my, you girls all look so glamorous as you get older. But your mother just keeps getting younger and younger." She and Mom laughed at that one.

Mrs. Selden always sends over extra bread and appetizers and extra desserts when we're there, and even before the waiter took our order, there was this really good cheese bread and riplets, which are these spicy crunchy fries, on the table.

Mom also ordered us sparkling water so that we'd "have something proper to toast with."

"To my best and most favorite girls in the world," she said, holding up her glass. "Who get more beautiful and whom I love more and more every day."

We all smiled and drank and I wondered if it was weird for Lindsay. I mean, Mom is *our* mom. Naturally she loves the three of us more than Lindsay, right?

Does Lindsay think that our mom loves her equally? I thought about this for a little while. Then the fried ravioli came and we all dived in.

Molly was telling a hilarious story about how someone stepped in doggie doo at the soccer game, which Mom kept saying was not appropriate dinner conversation, so Molly would stop. Then three seconds later she'd say, "So you want to know how it ends, right?" and she would tell a little more.

"Oh, I feel badly for the crew at the Park," said Mom, checking her phone under the table. "They really still have a ton to do to get ready for tomorrow."

"But this is our Family Fest!" I said.

"I know, I know, Kelsey," said Mom. "But here we are living it up, and poor Uncle Mike and Uncle Charlie are getting two hundred fifty donuts packed up for tomorrow! It doesn't feel right."

We finished dinner, and as we were all in a gooey-butter-cake coma, Molly said, "Hey, I have an idea. Let's stop by the Park and help out."

We all looked at each other.

"Well, is anyone tired?" asked Molly.

We all shook our heads.

"Let's do better than that," said Mom, with a

mischievous look in her eye. "Let's bring them dinner!"

"We're going to bring dinner to a restaurant?" asked Jenna.

"Yeah!" said Mom. "They won't have to cook it, so they'll be thrilled! Don't you know that's the secret of restaurants everywhere? Cook for people and they're happy!"

We ordered a ton of stuff off the menu to go. While we were waiting, Jenna said, "Okay, one last toast to the girls!" and raised her glass.

"I'm glad to be one of the girls tonight!" said Lindsay, raising her glass too.

I glanced over at her, and she was beaming from ear to ear. I realized that this was the happiest I'd seen Lindsay in a really long time. All of us were smiling and having fun and it didn't matter one bit that we had an extra person with us. Why did I ever get so upset about it? Family was family.

I raised my glass and said, "And one more . . ."

Everyone looked at me.

"Always additions," I said, looking at Lindsay and smiling. "They're better than subtractions. I'm really happy you're here with us, Lindsay."

"Cheers!" said Mom, and she gave me a little

wink. "More is always better. Always listen to the accountant when it comes to numbers."

"Or in this case, the accountant's daughter!" I said.

Mrs. Selden packed the food into to-go bags, and we piled into the car and headed back to Bellgrove.

We drove up to the Park and could see all the lights on and a lot of people walking around inside. Mom used her key and threw open the front door.

"The party is here!" yelled Molly.

Nans and Grandpa came out of the kitchen, and Uncle Mike, Uncle Charlie, and Dad all looked up. Then they saw that one of the things we'd brought was fried ravioli, and everyone grabbed plates and dug in.

"You're all dressed up!" said Nans. "Don't start packing things and moving things!"

"We can change!" said Jenna, and Mom ran us home and we all grabbed jeans and T-shirts.

When we returned we each took a job, either sorting and packing donuts or folding the menus that we were giving out with every purchase. There was something really fun about working on a project together, and everyone was playing music and singing as we worked an assembly line.

Finally we loaded everything into Uncle Charlie's

pickup truck and we were set. We drove home exhausted but excited.

It had been our second Family Fall Fest of the night, and I couldn't decide which one I liked better.

☀ ☀ ☀ ☀ ☀

Fall Fest starts off with a parade, and every year it's usually the sports booster club, the veterans' association, the town officials, and the dance squad who make their way down Main Street.

Since the sports booster club covers every sport that's played, it means every kid shows up in his or her uniform to march as well. The kids toss candy to the spectators lining the street. Everyone ends up at the festival part, which has different food stations, and booths that are sponsored by all the clubs and businesses in town. It's like a giant street fair.

We needed extra help during Fall Fest, so some of the field hockey team and the soccer team were helping at the Park's booth, which looked incredible thanks to Dad's frame and awning. The front of the booth actually looked like a real building, and it really stood out. Isabella, Hannah, and Sophia were behind the counter with me for my shift, and it was fun to work with my friends, except Isabella kept eating the donuts.

"Isabella!" I said. "You'd never last at Donut Dreams!"

"I know," she groaned. "But they are soooo good. Every time I have a bad day, my mom comes home with one of them for me!"

Olivia and Michelle came by for a visit and, of course, to have a donut.

"Donuts make you smile," said Sophia seriously.

"Maybe that should be our new slogan," I joked.

"Let's not talk about slogans," groaned Hannah. "We're still working on ours for the election. So far 'Two Girls Can Get It Done!' is still the most popular. But today I don't want to think about the election. Today I just want to have fun!"

"Okay, but just one suggestion," I said. "How about something like 'You Talk, We Listen'?"

"Hey," said Hannah. "That's good!"

"I love it!" said Olivia.

"Well, everyone appreciates it when someone listens, right? That's why Principal Clarke said they created the class reps. So everyone gets a chance to be heard."

"It's true," said Hannah. "That's really why I'm so interested in student council."

"It is?" said Olivia. "I thought it was that you just wanted to be in charge and make decisions."

"What?" said Hannah. "No, Isabella and I really share the same idea that we should be representing our class and helping to influence things that can make school a better experience for everyone."

Olivia looked like she was stewing for a second. "Well, sure . . . ," she said. "I knew Isabella felt that way. . . ."

Hannah gave her a strange look. "Sometimes you just have to let people know you're open to hearing them, and they'll tell you how they feel."

Olivia didn't say anything, and Sophia and I raised our eyebrows at each other.

We were selling jelly donuts and apple cider. "Come get your true red spirit!" we called as people lined up. The shift went by fast, and after we worked, we were able to walk around.

I waved to Principal Clarke, who was my new buddy, and went over to the town library's booth, where I took one of Ms. Castro's recommended reading lists. Some of the new titles looked so good, and I made a promise to myself to stop at the library soon.

At dusk we all made our way to the lake and spread out blankets. Sophia and Riley and I squeezed onto one, and Olivia and Isabella plunked onto another right next to us. Hannah and Elizabeth sat down on the other side, and Michelle wheeled herself next to me in her chair. I saw Lindsay sitting a few rows over, with Casey.

Lindsay looked up and rushed over to me, giving me a hug. "Are you mad that I'm not sitting with you?" she asked.

"Why would I be mad?" I said.

"Well, we're family," she said.

"True," I said, "but I'm not sitting with Molly or Jenna, and they're family."

"Yeah," said Lindsay. "I'm just always worried people will get upset. I mean, everyone has been so nice to me since Mom died, and sometimes I just want to be treated normally, not like I'm special or anything."

"We don't treat you specially," I lied.

"Well, usually you don't," said Lindsay. "And I appreciate that. I know you probably didn't want me around during your Family Fall Fest with your mom and sisters. I probably wouldn't have wanted me there either. But the thing is, I was glad that you thought it was okay to just be you and not treat me like I might break into a million pieces. It's hard to walk around and not want to snap my fingers at people and say, 'Act normal!'"

I blinked in surprise.

"Whew," she said. "I did not count on saying all that! But you're a good listener, and I guess mostly I just need someone to hear me."

I gave her a hug and said, "I am always here to listen to you. Now go back to your real BFF. I mean, if we're keeping it real, this blanket is full."

She laughed and said, "Meanie!" as she skipped back over to Casey.

I lay back and looked at the stars. It was a clear night, and it looked like the night sky had a million little glittering freckles. I thought about the last few weeks and how Dad and Jenna had listened to me, and about how my family always looked out for each other.

Maybe Principal Clarke was right. Maybe you didn't have to solve anything, you just needed to listen. And if it was as easy as that, maybe I was finally starting to figure this stuff out.

Chapter Thirteen
Family Is Everything

Mom and Dad and I had a talk after Fall Fest, and Mom told me that it was my turn to go to St. Louis, but they were also putting Lindsay in the rotation, and she would get the opportunity to go next.

I thought that sounded fair, and I knew that Lindsay would probably appreciate the time alone with Mom too.

"It was your mom's idea," Dad told me.

Mom and Dad looked at me, and I smiled. "Dad, you are a really good listener, but Mom is really good at solutions."

They both laughed.

Since Mom was speaking at the conference on the following Friday, she decided she would pick me

up right from school on Thursday, so we could drive
to St. Louis that afternoon.

After her presentation we'd drive home in time
for Family Friday dinner. I would finally have Mom
all to myself.

I had my bag packed Thursday morning before I
left for school, and I was so excited I could barely get
through the day.

☀ ☀ ☀ ☀ ☀

Before I knew it, it was time for Mom and me to hit
the road. We dropped off Molly and Mom gave Dad
a kiss goodbye.

"Knock those city folks dead, honey," he said, and
Mom hopped back into the car.

Soon we were on the highway and on our way.

"Ugh, this drive," Mom groaned. "This is how we
drove back and forth to school when I was in college.
I always hated this drive and I still do."

"Why?" I asked, looking around.

The trees were finally changing color, and the side
of the road looked like a yellow and orange rainbow.

"It's so boring!" said Mom. "I would count the
water towers to see how far away I was. We are four

water towers away from State. Unless they built some more lately . . ."

"I think it's relaxing to take a long drive," I said, settling back in my seat. "Are you nervous about your speech?"

"A little," said Mom. "I don't mind speaking in front of people, especially about what I know so well, but I get a little nervous that someone will tell me I'm wrong or I don't know what I'm talking about."

"But you do know what you're talking about! That's why they want you to speak as an expert!"

"I don't know everything, honey. I know what I know about our business. So I'm an expert on the Park, but outside that . . . I'm not so sure."

The Park was pretty successful, I guess. It had been around for fifty years. The food was always good and the people who worked there were always welcoming. I couldn't imagine it not being there.

"So if you didn't work at the Park, where would you work?" I asked, curious.

"Oh," said Mom. "Well, after college I was offered a lot of jobs in business."

"Like what?" I asked.

"Like in accounting offices in St. Louis, at an

investment firm in Chicago, and at a bank in New York. They were exciting job offers."

"Chicago? New York?!" I asked. "Really?"

"Yep," said Mom. "And I interviewed at all of them. I thought about each one. . . . Some were really good opportunities. It wasn't an easy decision."

"And?"

"And?" asked Mom. "Well, clearly I chose to come home and work for Grandpa and Nans at the Park."

"Why?" I asked, thinking about Mom living in Chicago or St. Louis. I couldn't even imagine her in New York.

"Well," said Mom, "you and I are a lot alike. I thought about what those jobs could offer me, and some of them were really interesting, big career paths. But in the end, I felt like I was happiest, and could be happiest, in Bellgrove. I wanted to come home."

"Did you regret it?" I asked, looking at her.

I never knew Mom even thought about living anywhere else. I was trying to think of her working for an investment firm, wearing a fancy suit and carrying a briefcase.

"Nope," said Mom. "Not a bit. Sometimes I wonder about choosing a different path. I mean, that's natural, but this is definitely where I want to be, and I'm lucky enough to be doing something I like very much with the people I love the most."

"Well, I'm glad at least you didn't go to California," I said. "Or New York or Chicago, for that matter."

Mom laughed. "No, I'm not a California girl. We'll have to see if Jenna is. Maybe she is and maybe she'll be back. I would not be unhappy if the three of you stayed in Bellgrove, but you each have to find the place that makes you happy."

We made it to St. Louis in time for dinner, but Mom wanted to check into the hotel first. We've stayed in hotels before for vacations, but we don't stay in them too often, and I'm always excited when we open the door and I get to see our temporary home. I checked out the fluffy beds and the view, then unwrapped the little soaps they give you in the bathroom.

Mom and I settled on a restaurant that was close to the hotel, so we walked over.

It was weird to be out to dinner with just Mom. First of all, when your family owns a restaurant, you don't eat in restaurants a lot. At home we mostly went out for tacos or sushi or pizza or Chinese food, since the Park didn't serve any of those types of food. Louie Louie was our special restaurant, but we only went there once or twice a year.

Mom ordered me something called a Shirley Temple, which tasted like ginger ale with cherry juice mixed in it and a cherry on top. It was delicious, and I felt very fancy and city-like.

"What are you thinking?" asked Mom, as I put my chin in my hand.

"I'm trying to remember the last time it was just you and me, without Molly or Jenna or Dad or anyone else," I said.

"When was it?" asked Mom.

"When I had strep throat over the summer and you took me to see Dr. Miller."

"Oh!" said Mom. She sighed. "That's not good. I wish I could do a better job of spending more time with each of you individually. You girls really need that."

I nodded.

"Well, now you have my full attention," she said. "So shoot. What do you want to talk about?"

"I don't know!" I said.

"Well, I want to know how middle school is," said

Mom. "Like, really want to know. Not just 'it's good.' I want to know how you feel about it. Give me some real feedback."

"Oh!" I said. "Well . . . it's actually okay. I mean, there have been some bumps. I'm friends with more people, I guess, which is good, and now I'm on the hockey team, which I like more than I thought I would. Plus, I'm the class representative, which I guess is pretty cool since people had to vote for me."

"It's very cool!" said Mom. "That's quite the vote of confidence from your peers!"

"I guess the best way to say it is that I'm finding my way," I said.

"That's exactly what you're supposed to be doing," said Mom. "No one knows their way directly. They don't call it middle school for nothing! You're in the middle of a lot of change and a lot of decisions. It takes some winding paths and some detours before you get on a road you feel is the right one. Just keep yourself open to people who want to help and are here to listen. You have to let them in."

I thought about that. So not knowing everything was okay. Not having solutions was okay.

"It's a lot, right?" said Mom. "But I don't worry

about you figuring out the right path. Just remember how kind you are. That's the key to everything. That kindness will always win out, and I know you'll stay true to yourself."

"You mean I won't be mean to my poor cousin?" I asked.

"Well, I hope you aren't mean to *anyone*," Mom said. "Jealousy is a real feeling. It's completely natural and totally understandable. Rather than squish it down, though, if you talk about it, you might feel better."

"So I'm supposed to say, 'Hey, Lindsay, I'm kind of jealous that everyone is looking out for you'?" I asked.

"Noooo," said Mom. "Well, maybe, if you said it a little more sensitively. And if you can't talk about it, then sometimes it's okay to just let that feeling be for a bit. Let's just say life is kind of like a jelly donut. Now the jelly is a sweet and delicious surprise when you bite into it, right?"

I nodded.

"But you don't always see it in there; it can be a surprise. And sometimes, if you bite it the wrong way, it spurts out all over you."

"Yeah, that happened the other day at work," I said. I shuddered a little as I remembered.

"Okay, I'm not going to ask why you were eating donuts at work," Mom said, giving me a look. "Sometimes life throws us a little. It's okay to be thrown and be uncertain and be a little squishy like jelly. Take your time. Listen to yourself. Eventually it will be okay. Jelly can be sticky, but it's rarely the end of the world."

We were talking so much that before I knew it, dessert was in front of us.

"Oh my goodness," said Mom. "This is the second time we're having butter cake in two weeks. This is not the healthiest eating we've done!"

"Oh, Mom," I said, with a mouthful of cake. "We sell donuts every day!"

"You got me on that one, kiddo," she said, and she stuck her fork in her cake.

※　※　※　※　※

The next morning I heard Mom blow-drying her hair after her shower, which she rarely did.

I got up and opened the curtains to let in the light.

Mom peeked out of the bathroom. "Oh, did I wake you?" she asked.

"No," I said. "I just woke up."

Mom wanted to get coffee and rehearse her presentation one more time before the conference, so I got dressed too. The plan was that I'd go with Mom and sit in the back of the meeting room (quietly, I'd promised!).

After Mom's meeting was over, we'd be able to go out and see the city a little bit before we headed back.

"Whoa . . . Mom!" I exclaimed as she came out of the bathroom.

Mom spun around so I could see her outfit from every angle, and I hardly recognized her. On most days she wore a button-up shirt, a blazer, and jeans to work, and depending on the season, either ballet flats or boots. She always looked cute, but definitely casual.

Today she was wearing a really nice black suit with a fancy patterned silk blouse under it, and black patent leather high heels. She had a really pretty necklace on that I hadn't seen her wear before, her hair was blown out, and she had on makeup. She looked amazing!

"I can polish myself up for the city!" Mom laughed.

"Wow. Let me take a picture!" I snapped her photo and sent it to my sisters.

> Check it out! Our cool, stylish mom is ready to fire up her speech!

In two seconds Molly texted back,

> Whoa. Are you sure that's our mother?

It would be another hour at least before Jenna even saw it.

Mom and I made our way to the meeting site, which was a big glass office building. I helped her set up her laptop and crawled under the table to plug in the cord, and she clicked through her presentation to make sure everything was reading on the big screen.

I looked at the rows of chairs and wondered if they'd all be filled, and within an hour, they were. Since I was all the way in the back, I could see how many people were in the audience. I hoped Mom wasn't too nervous.

If she was, you'd never know, because after she

was introduced, she strutted out like a pro and walked through the presentation. I couldn't follow everything she was talking about—lots of gobbledygook about profit and margins—but she spoke loudly and clearly and was even funny. At the end everyone applauded, but no one clapped louder than I did. After Mom's speech she had to stay and talk to a few people.

I stood a little off to the side and at one point Mom called me over and said, "This is my daughter Kelsey." And everyone made a fuss over me, told me I was pretty and how much I looked like my mom. It was a little embarrassing, but nice, too.

When everyone left, she said, "Okay, let's make a run for it!" and we ran back to the hotel, where she changed back to the mom I knew in less than five minutes.

"Ugh, I hate high heels!" she said, throwing them back into her suitcase.

"Do we have time to walk around a little?" I asked.

"We do!" said Mom. "Let's see the town."

We went wandering up and down the streets, popping in and out of all these cute clothing stores and a few antique stores. We found a shirt for Jenna, and a phone case that was just perfect for Molly. It was made out of soccer ball material. I saw a really pretty lavender scarf at this very sleek new boutique and picked it up.

"Do you like that?" asked Mom.

"Yes, but not for me," I said. "You know who would like this? Lindsay."

Mom nodded. "It would look great with her dark hair. And that's very sweet of you to think of her too."

We put all the bags into the car and Mom said, "Ready to say sayonara to St. Louis?"

"Yep," I said. "St. Louis is great, but take me home to good old Bellgrove!"

"Your wish is my GPS command!" said Mom, and she punched in HOME in the car system and off we went.

Mom had been right; it was a pretty boring ride, and I guess I was tired, because the next thing I knew, I woke up in our driveway.

"We're home!" I called as we stepped into the house.

"We missed you!" called Dad from the kitchen.

I sniffed. "Ooh, lasagna!" I said.

"No, my name is Dad, not lasagna," joked Dad, giving me a hug. "And yes, I made a giant lasagna to welcome you home."

"How'd it go?" he asked Mom, pulling her in for a kiss.

"She killed it," I said. "Mom is pretty impressive."

Dad laughed. "Yes, I know."

Mom peered in the oven. "Chris, how big is that lasagna? It's enough to feed an army!"

"You know who likes lasagna?" I asked, not even pausing. "Lindsay. And Uncle Mike and Skylar. If we have extra, should we invite them for dinner?"

Mom smiled. "Well, if you tell my brother there's lasagna, he'll be here in about three seconds."

I texted Lindsay,

> R u guys hungry? It's lasagna night! Come on over!

and sure enough, she immediately texted back,

> We're on our way!

I set the table for three more and thought, *Always additions.* I looked out the front window just as Uncle Mike pulled up to the house. I smiled and opened the door, eager to let my family in.

141

Still Hungry?
Here's a taste of the third book in the

series, Family Recipe!

Chapter One
Family and Friends

I threw down my bag, then I picked it up again and stuffed it into the cubbies that Dad had built us by the back door.

My sister Kelsey yelped, "Heeeeyyyy!" behind me when the door slammed before she got inside.

"Too slow!" I said and walked into the kitchen, kicking off my shoes.

"Too messy!" said Dad, pointing to my shoes. "In the cubby, please."

"Molly slammed the door on me," Kelsey whined behind me as she glared.

"Welcome home, girls!" said Dad. "It's nice to see you too!"

Dad had made us a platter of cheese and crackers and set it out on the kitchen counter. Kelsey and I dove for it hungrily.

"Did you eat lunch?" Dad said.

"Yeah," I said, stuffing a cracker in my mouth. "But that was like three hours ago."

"I miss snack time at school," said Kelsey.

"Kelsey, we haven't had snack time at school since kindergarten!" I pointed out.

"Well, they should have it in middle school," said Kelsey irritably, popping a cube of cheese in her mouth. "Everyone would be less cranky in the afternoon." She gave me an accusing look.

"I'm not cranky," I said, after I swallowed another mouthful of cheese and crackers. "I'm hungry."

"Okay," said Dad. "Eat your snack then let's see . . ." He walked over to the bulletin board in the kitchen where Mom kept all the calendars and schedules. "Molly, you have soccer at four thirty."

"Yep," I said, picking out two crackers and a bit

of cheese before making myself a mini sandwich. "I know."

"So that means homework needs to get started pronto," said Dad.

"Yep," I said again while devouring my mini sandwich. "I know."

"Kelsey, I need you to help Mom with dinner when she gets home from work," said Dad, still examining the bulletin board. "Wait, wait, you have hockey. Now how is this going to work . . . ?"

"Dad," said Kelsey, finishing off the last of the good crackers. "Mom went over it this morning. Jenna is driving me to hockey and you are taking Molly to soccer."

"Right!" said Dad, smacking his head. "I thought Jenna was working today, but she's just tutoring after school."

I went back to my cubby and took out my laptop and my Spanish book.

"What are you doing?" asked Kelsey.

"Starting my homework," I said, setting up at the table.

"Now?" asked Kelsey suspiciously.

"I have soccer in an hour and a half," I said. "And

hours of homework tonight, which is totally insane."

"You could start it when you get home from soccer," Kelsey said.

I rolled my eyes.

Kelsey is not entirely organized. My dad says Kelsey likes her downtime, but in reality, Kelsey just doesn't like to do homework. It's not that I like doing homework, but I honestly don't mind when it's interesting. The drill stuff, like my Spanish homework, is really annoying, so I like to just bang it out when I get home and get it over with. Kelsey would be whining about her French homework at nine o'clock tonight.

"Kelsey, why don't you take a page from Molly and get started too?" asked Dad.

Kelsey sighed dramatically.

Dad sighed dramatically back at her.

"How are we even related?" I grumbled and grabbed another cube of cheese.

"You have Mom's system-like approach," said Dad. "It's good that at least half the family has it."

I laughed. Mom and I are organized, and Jenna is too. Dad says that he and Kelsey, on the other hand, are "dreamers."

"So now Mom and dinner," said Dad, looking a little worried. "I was going to prep some veggies so she can make an egg dish but . . ."

"Mom and eggs," I reminded him, "are generally not a good pair."

"Definitely not," said Kelsey. "Remember when she tried to hard-boil them?"

Both of us started giggling. Even though Mom's family owns a restaurant, Mom cannot cook to save her life. She tried to hard-boil eggs to make egg salad once, and we still don't know what she did, but all the eggs started exploding. It was a huge mess. I'm pretty sure there's still some egg stuck on the ceiling over the stove.

My theory is that Mom senses us, especially when we talk about her. Just at that moment, the phone rang and sure enough, it was her.

Kelsey spoke to her first, going on and on about how ridiculous it was that she had so much homework.

I knew exactly what Mom was saying to her without even hearing it. *If you stop complaining and just do the homework, you'd be halfway done by now.*

Mom and I are a lot alike in that way. I have no time for drama or complaining.

Kelsey handed me the phone.

"Hi, honey," said Mom. "How was your day?"

"Fine," I said.

"Fine?" asked Mom, and I could tell she was wrinkling her face up.

"Yeah," I said. "You know it takes a few weeks to get into the swing of things with a new school year."

"That's true," said Mom. "Do you have a lot of homework?"

"While Kelsey was complaining, I got half of it done," I said, smirking as Kelsey stuck her tongue out at me.

Mom laughed. "You're just like me, kiddo!"

After I was done talking to Mom, I handed the phone to Dad, who talked to Mom for a few minutes and then said excitedly, "Hey girls, Grandpa made his famous chili at the restaurant today! Mom's bringing it home!"

"Dinner!" Kelsey yelled, punching the air.

"Yeah!" I yelled too.

Grandpa's chili was super delicious, so I was already looking forward to it even though my stomach was full of cheese and crackers. But I'd be hungry again after running around during soccer practice.

Dad smiled and nodded. He hung up and said, "Dinner is saved."

I knocked off most of my homework pretty quickly after that and went upstairs to get ready for soccer.

I started playing soccer when I was in kindergarten, and I've loved it ever since. I love how fast the game is, but I also love that there's a strategy. It looks like a crowd of people is just running around after a ball, but in reality, you have to have a plan to get the ball down the field. Everyone on the team has a specific role for moving the ball around.

I heard my older sister Jenna burst in the front door downstairs because Jenna doesn't do anything quietly. "I'm hooome!" she called.

"Start the parade!" Dad says like he always does.

Jenna is in high school, and she can drive, which she thinks makes her a lot cooler than she is, but she actually is pretty cool. She is also kind of intense. Mom says that Jenna is a "demon on the court" in tennis, which makes sense because Jenna is really competitive.

"Molly, ten-minute warning!" Dad called upstairs. "Soccer starts in twenty, and it takes ten to get there!"

I threw my hair in a ponytail and headed

downstairs. I didn't love having practice after school because I was already tired. We had it in the mornings the week before school started, which was better even though I had to streak myself beforehand with tons of sunscreen, making my eyes all stingy when I sweat.

"Hi, Molls," said Jenna, slamming the fridge. "Dad, what do we have for a snack? I'm starving."

Dad pushed the cheese and cracker plate towards her and Jenna scowled. "They ate all the good crackers!"

"There are bad crackers?" Dad said. "Huh. I didn't realize we could divide crackers into good and bad. That's good to know."

"Dad, you know what I mean!" Jenna fumed and opened the cabinet to rummage through it. She opened a box and popped a few crackers into her mouth.

"Eat some cheese and fruit with those," said Dad. "That's the healthy part."

"Dad, I am old enough to drive a car," said Jenna. "I know what healthy food is!"

Dad sighed and gave Jenna a hug. "You may be driving, but I will always see you as the toothless toddler who called herself Wenna because she couldn't say her Js yet."

I burst out laughing as Jenna rolled her eyes at him. Dad was so sentimental sometimes that we called him Mr. Goo.

"And *you*," said Dad dramatically, hugging me hard. "You were my baby who refused to say Dada or Daddy. That's the first word most kids say! But not you. It was Mama Mama Mama. Then Wenna. Then dog . . ."

I was laughing because I knew the rest. "Then 'kit cat' for Henry the cat," I said.

"Yes!" said Dad. "Henry, then Daddy. Finally! You nearly killed me!"

I smiled. We actually have a video of me sitting on Dad's lap before I touched his nose and said "Daddy" for the first time. He was so happy he looked like he was going to cry.

"Sorry about that," I said, then hoisted my soccer bag over my shoulder.

"Okay. My child who now loves me has soccer," Dad said to Jenna. "Kelsey is . . . where is Kelsey? Kelsey?" he bellowed upstairs. "Are you on the phone before you finished your homework?"

"Probably," said Jenna, smirking.

Kelsey came downstairs looking guilty. "I had to

ask Lindsay what the assignment was," she said.

"Kelsey . . . ," Dad warned.

"Fine, I'll start my homework."

"Great!" said Dad. "Jenna will take you to hockey while I take Molly to soccer. Okay, kiddo," he said to me, and we headed out to the car.

Even though I've been sitting in the front for a long time now, it still feels weird to ride next to Dad in the front seat.

"You excited about the game this weekend?" Dad asked.

"Yeah," I said, "but the first game of the season is always hard. There are some different girls playing this year."

"That's expected," Dad said. "That's why you have practice, to get to know each other's strengths and rhythms."

"Yeah," I said and rested my head against the window.

One of the good things about Dad is that he understands that even though I like to talk, I also like to be quiet at times. Jenna talks nonstop and Kelsey is either talking or texting and we can all be a little noisy, but sometimes I like to zone out, especially when I'm getting ready for soccer. It kind of clears my head so I can focus. Mom used to joke that I had an on and off switch and nothing in between.

Dad pulled into the lot at the soccer field and we got out of the car.

I guess it's kind of weird that Dad still comes to my practices now that I'm in middle school. I noticed the other day that most kids get dropped off, but Dad sits in the bleachers, watching. He's not one of those parents who yells from the sidelines, which I am very thankful for, but he definitely pays attention.

"Okay," he said, taking his coffee mug. "I'll be in the stands if you need me, honey. Have a great practice!"

I waved and trotted off to the sidelines.

My BFF Madeline was on my team. And this year, Riley and Isabella were playing with us too, which was both good and weird. Good because I liked them both, but weird because Riley was better friends with Kelsey than me.

Coach Wendy had us out on the field before I could think about it too much. We warmed up and did some drills, then she had us count off for a few three-on-three scrimmages. I liked those because if you have a full team on the field, you aren't always on the ball. When it's just the three of you, it can be much more intense.

Madeline was on my squad. We've been best friends since preschool and we've been playing together forever, so I know almost without thinking which way she's going on the field or when she'll decide to take a shot.

We were passing the ball back and forth pretty well when Riley said, "Hey guys, I'm on your side," which startled me a little.

I nodded and passed to her, and she tripped over the ball. Her face got red, and she said, "Sorry," and looked down at the ground.

Riley is a good player, but when she thinks people are watching or there's a clutch moment, she sometimes just whiffs on the ball.

"It's okay," I said. "Let's work you in better."

I nodded toward Madeline and she nodded back.

"Play forward," I said to Madeline and then I passed the ball up the field to her.

She made a really nice kick to Riley, who sank it in the goal.

"Now that's it!" called Coach Wendy happily.

"That's it, that's it, girls! I saw what you did there. Worked each other in and figured out how to play together. Great job!"

Riley took a bow, and I laughed. I looked up at Dad, who gave me a thumbs-up and a grin.

We played for another thirty minutes before Coach Wendy blew the whistle.

"Girls," she said. "This weekend is our first game. I don't care if we win."

Everyone looked at each other.

"I care that you play well as a team," Coach Wendy explained. "We have a long season and plenty of games to win, but let's do this as a team, okay?"

We all nodded.

"Now give me a G!"

"G!" we all yelled.

"What's that for?"

"Go!" we yelled.

"G is for?" she said, smiling.

"Great!" we yelled.

"G is for?"

"Goal!" we yelled.

"Go! Great! Goal!"

I wondered if I was the only one to realize that

the cheer didn't exactly make sense, but it sure got us all riled up.

Once I sank into the seat in the car, I realized how tired I was. "Oof," I said. "That knocked me out."

"Well, you did a heck of a lot of running," said Dad.

"Speaking of running, did you get a chance to run today?" I asked him.

Usually he went in the morning but once school started, it was harder for him to get out in time.

"Nah, I missed today," Dad said, wincing. "And I definitely feel it."

"There's a track around the soccer field," I said, thinking about it. "When you bring me to practice, you can just do some laps instead of sitting in the bleachers."

"What, you don't like your old dad sitting around watching you?" Dad joked.

"Dad," I said, already knowing where this was going. "I like having you at practice. I want you to be at practice. But I also know how much you like to run."

Dad smiled. "Ah, okay. I thought you were trying to nicely tell me you were too old to have your dad with you! I thought maybe I embarrassed you."

"I know," I said and rolled my eyes. "Mr. Goo, you are very sensitive!"

Dad laughed. "You know what Mr. Goo who is sensitive wants?"

"What?" I asked as we turned onto our street.

"Some chili!" he said. He pointed to Mom's car, which was in front of us.

"Then step on it, sir," I said. "Because if we don't get home soon, the rest of the family is going to eat it all! Follow that chili!"

"Give me a C!" said Dad.

"C!" I said.

"Wait, we don't have time to spell out chili," said Dad. "How about just 'go'?"

"You know, maybe we should say 'give me a G' for Grandpa," I said, picking up my bag. "Go Grandpa for saving us from Mom's dinner!"

Dad cracked up and said, "Let's keep that cheer between us."